UNCHIPPED: WILLIAM

THE UNCHIPPED SERIES
THE MEETING: AN UNCHIPPED SHORT STORY
UNCHIPPED: KAARINA
UNCHIPPED: WILLIAM
UNCHIPPED: ENYD
UNCHIPPED: LUNA
UNCHIPPED: THE RESORT
CHIPPED: LAURA
CHIPPED: DENNIS
CHIPPED: MARGARET
CHIPPED: JOVAN
CHIPPED: THE REVENANT
DECHIPPED: KRISTIAN
DECHIPPED: MARIA
DECHIPPED: OWENA
DECHIPPED: IRIS
DECHIPPED: THE DOWNLOAD
RECHIPPED: CITY OF SERBIA
RECHIPPED: CITY OF ENGLAND
RECHIPPED: CITY OF CALIFORNIA
RECHIPPED: CITY OF FINLAND
RECHIPPED: THE BUTTON

COMING SOON!
THE MACHINA DEUS SERIES (2024)
SERF GIRL
FAMA GIRL
SLUM GIRL

UNCHIPPED: WILLIAM

TAYA DEVERE

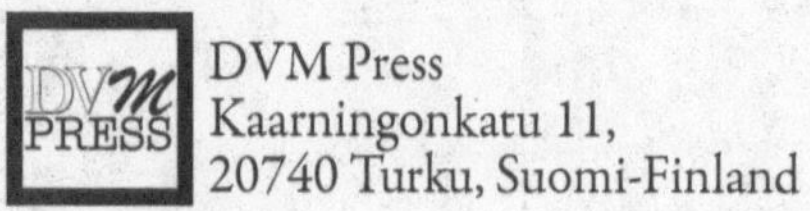

DVM Press
Kaarningonkatu 11,
20740 Turku, Suomi-Finland

www.dvmpress.com
www.tayadevere.com

For information about special discounts available for bulk purchases, sales promotions, fund-raising and educational needs, contact sales@dvmpress.com

ISBN 978-952-7404-05-8 First Ebook Edition
ISBN 978-952-7404-06-5 First Print Edition

Cover Design © 2020 by Deranged Doctor Design - www.derangeddoctordesign.com

Cover Spine Design © 2022 by Chris DeVere

Editing by Christopher Scott Thompson, Lindsay Fara Kaplan, and Elle Fort

To all underdogs out there:
The black sheep, the odd ducks, the rejects, the loners.
You make this world go around.

CONTENTS

SHORT STORY

THE MANSION 1

UNCHIPPED: WILLIAM

CHAPTER 1
THE FARM...25

CHAPTER 2
CITY OF CALIFORNIA....................................55

CHAPTER 3
2 YEARS EARLIER 87

CHAPTER 4
BETWEEN THE AVOCADO TREES............... 109

CHAPTER 5
DOWN THE STREAM 141

MY DEAREST READER 177

ABOUT THE AUTHOR.................................... 179

FINAL THANKS 181

THE MANSION

A short story in the world of the Unchipped series

Outside City of California, 2086

Two duffel bags hit the floor with a dull *thump*. Trying his best to ignore his wildly beating heart, William hopes no one will be able to see the anxiety beneath his calm and collected demeanor.

He wants to ignore it all.

The throbbing pain under his strategically positioned locks.

The itching scab over the small, shaved spot on the back of his skull.

The fact that he's here, outside the neon-green city.

It all reminds him of the failure he's become.

Bill steps away from the duffel bags and looks around the mansion's entrance hall. He's never visited this place before. White walls, white floor tiles, and a high ceiling make the large space seem almost endless. A spiral staircase rises from the farthest corner. Behind the stairs, he sees an open kitchen area with an enormous kitchen island, with dozens of avocados and oranges scattered along three long counters.

A massive ceiling fan whirs above his head, its giant blades moving the air through the empty hallway.

Kaarina? You there? William taps for his newfound friend. A girl—a woman—far away from here.

How it's possible for him to enter another Unchipped mind, to talk to her from across the world, is beyond him. They have no idea how the two of them are connected, able to see and hear each other's thoughts and surroundings as long as they both tune in at the same time.

Their regions are unsafe for different reasons.

Like a sick mind game, Bill plays with the thought of living where Kaarina lives: in the eastern part of the world, where his worst enemy would be his own mind, where the mass suicides have wiped out ninety percent of the population of what is now called "East-Land."

As dumbfounding as it seems, he's better off here in the West, where the enemy roams free instead of inside his head. On the streets, at the parks, in the suburbs. Armed and unstable, the hostile and the suspicious ready to shoot first and ask questions never. The enemy here is everyone else, those who used to be labeled as "upstanding citizens."

Outside the green city, those who are not eligible to live inside the electric fences fight or flee for their lives. Only a single city has access to the Happiness-Program and its augmented reality. A mere one percent of what used to be called a state. Those outside the fences can trust no one. Only someone with a death wish would try to live in the empty houses. The aisles of an empty grocery store could easily become a final resting place. A conversation with another person could end with a bullet in the head.

All those living outside the city have gone rogue in one way or another. Not all of them take part in the mass-shootings, but those who don't carry a gun must now run from those who do. Thousands have committed suicide. The rest are constantly in search of remote places where they can hide. Just like Bill. Though he has options—more so than most. And he's chosen to work for a shady business that he knows nothing about, rather than live out on the streets. The thought of holding a gun—let alone firing one to take a life—turns his stomach.

Bill was supposed to be one of the lucky ones. In a way, he still is. He'd be living in the city right now if not for an unfortunate mismatch between the micro-chip and his brain. The chip is still there, installed and ready, but instead of integrating him into the city's Chip-System, it had made him physically ill. It wasn't until he had walked all the way to the electric fencing, asked a guard to open the main gate, and stepped out into the desert that the pounding headache had finally stopped.

A lucky coincidence then got him a job interview in an odd, isolated community up in the mountains. After Bill's chipping failed, one of his networking contacts, now retired in the city, told Bill about an unusual-sounding business looking to hire a graphic designer. The live-in position would give him something to do and a safe place to live while he waits for the Chip-Center to figure out what went wrong with his brain implant. He drove up the same evening, spent his night in the woods where no one would see him, and waited for dawn to come. There he alternated between light sleep and fearful wakefulness, staring at his car parked by the road near the mansion's metal gates. If someone were to break into it or steal it, there was nothing he could do but watch.

The gates opened in the morning, and he drove into a luxurious farm with pools, an old horse stable, and endless rows of avocado and orange trees. He should be happy to be here, privileged, but in the back of his mind, a shameful feeling of dissatisfaction won't let him be.

Because, yes, he *should* be safely tucked away from the murdering outcasts, but not on this farm with its white mansion. He should be inside City of California, munching on vegan-nuggets and chit-chatting with those who are worthy of being a part of humanity's second chance.

Instead, he's here, inside this huge, white building, far from the city and its surrounding madness.

Footsteps echo from upstairs. A barefoot woman, short and lean, but strangely rugged, makes her way down the spiral staircase. She's wearing AR-glasses and talking through the integrated microphone: technology to be used only inside the green city fences. Bill doesn't know much, but he knows gadgets like that should not exist outside the city limits. Not here, up on the mountainside, high above the chaos and echoing gunshots. How did she get her hands on the *glasses*?

The woman either misses Bill completely, or she simply chooses to ignore him. Her smooth, catlike steps lead her to the kitchen. Two industrial refrigerators take up most of the side wall. Under the long counter spaces: cupboards and drawers, dishwashers and laundry machines.

The dark-skinned woman grabs an orange and digs for something in one of the endless white drawers. Then she sits on a barstool at the kitchen island. A small paring knife sinks into the orange peel.

Bill follows her into the kitchen. Working in perfect harmony, the knife and her thumb peel off pieces of orange and pop them into her mouth. The woman eats without a word, still oblivious to the stranger standing in front of her. Though the call has seemingly ended, she hasn't taken the AR-glasses off.

Finally, her dull-sounding voice breaks the silence between them. "Bodyguard or graphic designer?"

First, surprise. Then annoyance. Bill's body tenses from the agitation, or maybe it's because of his night spent lying uncomfortably in the woods. He stares at the clearly bored woman. What a jerk. The disinterested look on her face tempts him to turn around, collect his bags, and drive out of the fenced-in twenty-five-acre farm.

Then, the muffled sound of explosions echoes from somewhere in the distance and he's stuck again, standing there at this stranger's mercy. He has nowhere else to go. This is it. It feels weird to talk to anyone, unsafe, but Bill's connection had told him this place was run by somewhat stable human beings. Whatever that means these days.

He finally spreads his arms and gestures for the woman to look at him. "Do I look like a bodyguard to you?"

She takes a moment to investigate Bill's appearance. Whether it's his tall, slim build, the carefully manicured nails, or his bundle of locks covering the shaved patch where his chip was installed, he doesn't know, but the woman finally nods and smiles.

She takes off the AR-glasses, pops the last piece of fruit in her mouth, and tosses the knife into one of the kitchen sinks. "Gotcha. Follow me." Making a beeline for the two duffel bags, the woman picks them up and throws them over her shoulder. Her frame should be too petite to be this strong, her body too lean to lift the heavy bags with such ease.

Her steps spiral up the staircase, her bare feet flapping softly against the stairs' wooden surface. Bill hurries after her. Upstairs, he follows the woman into a dimly lit hallway with an endless row of closed doors on each side. Just to his right, though, one door is open. He walks in and finds the bull-strong woman holding one of his sketchbooks. The duffel bags lie on the king-sized bed, one of them unzipped.

A few long strides and Bill snatches the notepad from the invader's hands. "What are you doing? That's private!"

The woman shrugs and turns away. "I thought I'd save us some time and see where we're at. I'm hoping that's not your best work." She walks to a set of silky white curtains and pushes them aside. She opens the double doors that lead onto a balcony as large as the spacious bedroom Bill now stands in. A warm puff of air flows in. It must be a hundred degrees outside.

"Gets a bit stuffy in here. I meant to air it out after your predecessor left the other day, but I guess I forgot."

"Did you also forget that I haven't even accepted the job yet? That this is supposed to be an interview, not some rude-ass welcome party?"

Her harsh laughter fills the room. "My bad, bud. The name is Maria. I guess I sort of run this shit-show, or at least get the newbies settled in. No one's really in charge here and I'd be shocked if you see anyone besides me and Micky."

"And who's Micky?"

Maria ignores his question and gestures around the room. "This here will be your bedroom. Guests are obviously not allowed, and you'll need to apply for a permit to leave the premises. The art studio is attached, just through that door," she nods at a sliding door to her right, "and the bathroom's over there," a nod to her left, "and as you already know, the kitchen's downstairs."

She stops for a second and peeks at Bill from under her brows. When he doesn't say anything, Maria continues. "Gallons of water are stocked in the hall-way pantry. Take as many as you need but log the amounts on the pantry's electric pad. It's screwed into the closet door, you'll see. I've labeled a shelf for you in one of the fridges, but I suggest you write your name on everything. Unmarked goods are known to disappear around here. Any gadgets you need for your work?"

Bill rubs the bridge of his nose. Does she have to be so intense? So clearly in a hurry to get rid of him? "I'm sorry . . . gadgets?"

Maria points at the sketchbook Bill still holds in a tight grip. "You'll need to submit your work, right? Hard to do that with a piece of paper. As much as I admire your old-fashioned ways, the client won't be interested in a paper version. And maybe it's best if this particular piece never sees daylight, anyway. I suggest you toss it down the trash chute in the studio so we can burn it downstairs."

Bill lifts the notepad to see which piece Maria's so eager to burn. It's one of his latest sketches: a green-glowing digital box with the letters "S.C.A.M." printed on its side. A product of his latest mood episode.

As if she's reading his mind, Maria says, "Now if I understand correctly, you're going through the same, um . . . *stages* as the previous designer. What is your current status?"

"My what?"

Maria sighs and runs her hand across her shaved head. Perhaps she once had long, wavy hair. Why didn't she grow it back after the failed procedure?

A fine scar, long healed, is just visible on the back of her skull.

"Let me rephrase that. Are you able to work, bud? A new order just came in last night. Tons of Chip-Cart objects needed in the city. And I hate to break it to you, but after Tom fled into the city, you're the only in-house designer we have."

Bill tosses the sketchbook on top of the open duffel bag. "Of course I'm able to work. I've got it under control."

Maria shrugs, as if to tell him that she doesn't really care. She starts toward the door, clearly eager to get away from her newest roommate—the newest "bud." As she strolls by, adjusting the hem of her shirt, Bill notices the gun at the small of her back. Up until now it had been hidden by her oversized flannel shirt. Why does she need to carry a weapon when there's a guard outside—and who wears flannel in this weather?

"Oh, that's what you're worried about? Her choice of outfit?"

Exhausted by all the information Maria's already thrown at him, Bill ignores Kaarina's mocking words.

"Pills or meds, technology and devices, food and black-market goods, you come to me. Anything else, there's another pad on the fridge door. Just add the items there and the crew will bring in your order in two to three business days. Help yourself to all the fruit you can bear to eat. Any questions?"

"Ask about the gun. What if she's one of the crazies?"

Anyone not willing to defend themselves is crazy, Kay. It is what it is.

But deep inside, Bill agrees with her. You would need to be out of your mind to kill another human being. Or is it the killing that drives them crazy afterward? Bill doesn't ever want to find out.

He scans the white room and then stops at the view that opens up beyond the balcony door. Mountains and desert surround a green-glowing city, tucked in an expanse of endless nothingness. The explosions and gunfire can no longer be heard.

Maria shifts her weight from one foot to another and clears her throat. "Bud? Questions?"

"Just one. I told Texas I would come and take a look. That I'd decide later. How are you so sure I'll stay here? That I'll accept the job?"

Maria reaches for the doorknob. Before leaving Bill alone in his new home, she says, "Because you'd have to be a complete dumbass not to."

The electric pen glides smoothly along the surface of the drawing tablet. A rush of creativity has taken over Bill's mind—a seamless flow, blocking away Kaarina, the outer world, and his new community. It's just him, the pen, and the buzz that is his mind.

At first, he thought he wouldn't be able to fill the order. It came directly from the head of the green city, but the items on the list felt too absurd—just plain ridiculous—for any adult human to desire.

A brimmed hat, the size of an umbrella.

A winter coat made out of neon-colored feathers.

A watch to wear on your forehead.

Block shoes with five small snake heads.

Crossbred pets in all the colors of the rainbow: a cat-rabbit, a miniature poodle-pony, a lion-monkey...

Right after his first lonely breakfast in the shared kitchen, Bill had started in on the weird clothing accessories. He was hoping that by the time he got to the end of the list, he'd find some sort of sense in what he was designing. By the time he started his first drawing, an orange poodle-pony, his hand and the electric pen had taken on a shared new life of their own.

"What on earth is that supposed to be?"

It's odd for Kaarina to reach out to him so much. She's been popping in and out of his mind all morning. Most of the time it's Bill who barges into her mind without warning. They have no idea why the two of them are connected, or even how they are connected. All they know is that it has something to do with their malfunctioning chips.

"It's a poodle-pony . . . " Bill mumbles, refusing to focus on the absurdity of his work. A black, two-fingered smudge guard on his left hand, he keeps the pen going and his mind on the task.

"Is it supposed to be a pet?"

"Beats me."

"Maybe it's some sort of weird sex thing they have going on in the city."

Bill grunts under his breath and moves on to the next item on his to-do list: an invisible, pear-shaped backpack.

"And here I thought the digital-dog walkers in City of Finland were a bit out there. Your city is way crazier."

He doesn't reply, hoping that the woman in his head will finally take the hint and leave him be. After a minute of peace, Bill thinks his silent treatment has worked.

"If the backpack's supposed to be invisible, how can you even draw it?"

The pen drops onto the tablet. "Who the fuck cares, okay? Who cares what those numbnuts do with all this crap? They stroll around their stupid city, in their stupid green-screen coveralls, wearing this nonsense and thinking they look cool or hip or whatever-the-fuck the cool kids call it these days."

He picks up the pen to finish his work. The plastic tip hovers on the screen but the flow is gone. Bill takes off the smudge guard and tosses it on the desk, along with the pen. "You happy now? I'm one item away from submitting this motherfucker, and now I can't bring myself to draw another line. I mean, you're right. How the fuck am I supposed to draw something *invisible*? But I have to if I want the CCs. If you ask me, fifty chip-credits for this stupid shit is ludicrous. But hey, it's their money. And I'll be rich again."

Bill gets up and paces around the studio. "But will I be cruising along the Pacific Coast Highway in my brand-new Aston-Martin? Oh no. No, no, no, no, no. I'll be stuck here, working for some bigshot in the city that hasn't even bothered to introduce himself after hiring me. But hey! I got all-you-can-eat avocados and oranges. Who am I to bitch about life?"

He stops near the studio door as a man carrying a pair of AR-glasses approaches. His name is Miguel, and they met this morning back in the kitchen, where Bill was seated at the counter eating an orange. He sat down nearby, told Bill to call him Micky, and informed him that the two of them were "playing on the same team." Bill has always hated that saying, but something about the way Micky carried himself, or maybe it was his friendly, genuine smile, had made Bill instantly forgive him for using such a worn-out cliché.

Now Micky stands in the middle of the room, unsure where to set his gaze. His loose surf-shorts and T-shirt make him look like a lost tourist without a map, desperately trying to find his way back to the hotel. But Micky won't be staying in any hotels anytime soon. Just like everyone else here, he's stuck living on this remote farm—though his job running errands does get him out of the house way more than most of the people living here.

"Sorry, should I come back later?" Micky points at the door but keeps his friendly eyes on Bill.

"No, it's okay. Just a small argument with my, um..."

Micky raises his eyebrows, still pointing at the door. "Long-distance boyfriend?"

Kaarina's fine blond hair and forest-green eyes flash through Bill's mind. The connection's long gone. She must have stopped tapping him as soon as he started ranting.

"It's a girl. Someone I met on the day I was chipped."

Micky doesn't try to hide his surprise. "Oh wow! Glad to hear at least some of us are brave enough to use our . . . abilities. You'll need to tell me how you got another Unchipped to respond to your tapping. No one will let me in." He walks over and hands Bill the AR-glasses. "But first, you have an AR-call."

Bill takes the glasses and frowns. "From whom?"

"It's Texas, the boss. He would like to welcome you to the farm."

The metal railing feels cool under Bill's arms, as he breaks into a nervous sweat. With the AR-glasses on, it's like he's suddenly been thrown back into the green city. He stares at glowing palm trees, half-naked holograms, and reflective billboards advertising the newest Happiness-Pill and its "secret twist." It's a trailer, or a screen saver, that people who are not connected with the augmented reality are forced to watch during an AR-call.

Bill refocuses on his new boss's Texan accent echoing in his ears. The glasses make it seem that the voice is coming from inside his head. For a moment he wonders if the chip in his brain has suddenly started to work. But if it did, he'd be in the green city sipping margaritas, not out here in the middle of nowhere, leaning against a metal balcony railing with a cigarette butt between his fingers. Two, maybe three puffs—that's all he'll get out of it. Still, it's better than nothing. Tobacco is the first thing he'll buy on the black market, as soon as he finishes drawing the cursed backpack so he can get paid.

"I believe that's all there is to know, my friend. Maria kind of runs the household now, though no one's really in charge. I try and visit once or twice a year, but traveling is kind of a burden these days."

Bill imagines an overweight, naturally bald, seventy-something man, sucking on a Cuban cigar, sunken into a leather gaming chair by a green-glowing pool. Bill can almost hear him licking his greasy fingers after finishing his nightly five-course vegan meal.

Texas has just finished explaining how he didn't want the mansion to go to waste, even after he retired and moved into the city. Running the business had almost put him into an early grave, but at the same time, the thrill of it all was the single thing keeping him alive.

Bill wonders if the man has a family, but something about his new boss tells him it's not wise to be the one asking the questions. Besides, it's a rare thing for people to have a romantic companion in their lives these days. It's even rarer to have children.

In this whole conversation, Bill has asked only one question: what business are they in, exactly? A dozen people in the mansion work for Texas, yet Bill has no idea what it is they do.

After a break of a few seconds, Texas's voice rumbles through the invisible earpiece. "Don't worry too much about that, my friend. We move all kinds of goods. I guess you could call us a luxury brokerage of sorts, if I had to put a label on it."

What kind of a businessman can't name the industry he works in?

The man clears his throat before continuing. "I do have one more question for you. It's not about your design work; you're the best of the best, or so I was told. You'll deliver what's needed, I'm sure."

"I'll have the first order ready by tomorrow morning."

"Good, good. Excellent. I was also told you have an impressive network from your previous life. Tell me, William, any connections to the East-Land?"

Kaarina's thick accent echoes in his ears, but it's just a memory. She hasn't checked in since Bill went off on her earlier for ruining his creative Zen state. Over a freaking make-believe backpack.

"Connections, sir?"

"Yeah, you know, business acquaintances, family members, long-distance . . . um . . . relations?"

"No, not really. Or . . . I do talk to this Unchipped woman in City of Finland from time to time. But she's a nobody, lives in the woods with a bunch of wild animals. Like actual animals, not the suburban folks that harass her for the meat and stolen goods that she gets from . . . "

Stop talking Bill, he thinks to himself, but the words keep coming. As soon as he told the man about Kaarina, he knew it was a bad idea. He shouldn't be so trusting. Not even with the man who would soon make him very wealthy.

Bill can't live in the city—thanks to his uncooperative brain and the microchip installed on its cortex—but he refuses to be gunned down in the streets either.

He's had to give away his freedom, at least parts of it, but he'll get to live in this mansion, eat fresh food and drink pure water. No matter the absurdity of the items that the city orders and then sells on the Chip-Cart program, Bill's once again doing the work that he loves.

He'll soon have more CCs than he can spend at the black market or in the city.

No gunman can enter this fenced-in farm with twenty-four seven surveillance.

He's among other people. True, like most people these days, his roommates choose to stay behind closed doors. Other than Maria and Micky, Bill hasn't even seen any of the other tenants.

This is not ideal, but it's the next best thing.

"Well, I'll be damned. Might come in handy one day, this little connection of yours. City of Finland happens to be the headquarters of the Happiness-Program. No shootings there, easier to keep things in order."

In his mind's eye, Bill sees the Chip-Center Kaarina ran away from in the middle of the night, nothing but thin hospital pajamas covering her pale Nordic skin.

Shivers run down his spine. A bad feeling crawls up from his stomach and sticks in his throat. Something's off, but he's not sure whether he wants to learn what it is.

"Well, my friend. I'll let you go. Almost bedtime. By the way, did Maria fill you in on the night shifts?"

Bill shakes his head to bring himself back to this time and place. "Night shifts, sir?"

"Oh, Maria, Maria. There's no one I'd rather have beside me in a fist fight, but when it comes to simple things like filling in the newbies . . . "

The bad feeling burns in Bill's throat, suffocating him.

"Well, no big deal. I'm letting you know now. And it goes without saying, each night shift comes with a hefty bonus. One hundred CCs for six hours of patrolling."

"Patrolling for what, sir?"

The sound of a gas lighter fills Bill's ears while he waits for Texas to explain the reason behind this nauseating feeling in his gut.

"You already mentioned them, the animals that lurk around the suburbs and other areas. The outcasts that live outside the city."

"Oh. But I was talking about City of Finland, sir. Those people over there are harmless, just hobos living in the woods."

"You might be talking about City of Finland, but I'm talking about City of California. The animals they have in the east are very different from the ones we get out here. Our beasts have guns . . . and minds gone rogue."

Bill slides his back down the balcony railing until he's sitting down on the concrete floor. He's tempted to toss the AR-glasses over the edge. Let them crash against the pavement bricks in the front yard.

But then he'd be homeless. Jobless. Futureless.

"Yup. Those suckers should know by now. My land is not to be messed with. But not to worry, my friend. Word travels fast. We hardly get any intruders these days."

It sounds like Texas is blowing the cigar smoke straight into Bill's ear and from there into his panicking brain. The smoke lingers, suffocating, intoxicating, ruining the images of a not perfect, but better tomorrow.

"Yeah, my friend. Any time you see those thieving scavengers around my fences, you take care of it."

"How do you mean, sir?"

"On my goddamn property, you let your gun do the talking."

2

WILLIAM

December 2088
West-Land, City of California

CHAPTER 1
THE FARM

Two hummingbirds take off from the porch of the mansion. With a coffee mug in his hands, Bill steps outside into the early morning sun. He doesn't bother with shoes, not even after Micky nearly stepped on a rattlesnake just outside the mansion's parking lot. "Can you imagine? In the middle of freaking December," he had huffed while telling Bill what had happened. He had flung himself onto Bill's king-sized bed like he owned the damn thing.

For anyone, this view, this house, and this farm would seem like a dream. The impossible becoming possible. A winning lottery ticket. A third chance in life. Anyone living here would walk outside, their footsteps light. They'd choose to focus on the glorious morning sun. Ignore the distant gunshots and echoes of screams. Close their eyes and think, *"I must be the luckiest person alive after The Great Affliction."*

Anyone but Bill.

He used to have a house much like this. Not a mansion in San Diego, but something better. Up in the green hills of Los Angeles. His apartment had a pool twice the size of the drained one that sits in the mansion's courtyard to his left. Two cars, sometimes three. All the latest gadgets. So many 3D printers he'd lost count. Art worth millions of dollars. He used to be important. Someone special.

Not a graphic designer-slash-CEO working for the man. Not a survivor with a sliced and flawed brain and a faulty chip. Not a grown-ass man still living with roommates.

The hard ground and fine sand used to feel foreign under Bill's feet. Until two years ago, he had never lived in the countryside, on a farm, or anywhere except among tall buildings and four-lane highways.

He stands in the middle of the mansion's driveway, sips his coffee, and stares at the orange trees lining up just beyond the wire fence that rises around their living quarters. A cut hole gives them access to the orange and avocado groves. Another hole has been cut in the fence at the back of the premises. This is where they come in, the trespassers. The scavengers cut that hole a long time ago, but the mansion's security guard, Earl, insists it not be fixed. When asked why, he mumbles something about a funnel.

The end of Earl's funnel is where Micky saw a trailer arrive last night, just as he finished another uneventful round of night patrol. Of course, Micky should have dealt with the trespassers when he saw them. But who is Bill to judge him for not wanting to kill another innocent man? They all guess but no one knows for sure; the only one who actually kills trespassers is Earl. And maybe Maria, though it's not like her to kiss and tell.

Behind the house and down a slope, three metal horse barns fall into disrepair. Empty and useless, the stable is now home to rats, mice, and the damn rattlesnakes. There they build their nests and other comfy hiding places inside fifty spacious horse stalls.

"Filthy little creatures," he mumbles, but isn't sure whether he's talking about the rodents or people like Earl, killing animals just for the fun of it. Whenever he hears Earl shooting the critters down there—just for his personal entertainment—a lump rises in Bill's throat. Just because they're repellent doesn't mean they need to die.

Ahead in front of the house rises an endless row of orange trees. Somewhere out there—more than five acres out—the oranges change into avocados. Some of the fruit gets collected, but most of it falls and rots on the ground.

To Bill's left, beyond the pool, are the mansion's parking lot and the metal gates, generally guarded by Earl. Next to the gates stands the guard's shed. This is where Earl spends most of his time reading historical fiction and absently fingering one of his many weapons. That's all he ever does. That is his life. Was he like that before? When they all still enjoyed things like traveling, social gatherings, and privacy? Bill's never asked. Most nights, Earl falls asleep in his little shed and wakes up in the morning with his open book stuck to his forehead.

Wings whistle with a slow, droning buzz as a red and green hummingbird hovers around one of the feeders. Bill watches as a thin beak sinks into a red plastic flower.

Is it the redhead, Melissa, who fills the feeders? Must be. Who else would use perfectly good sugar to feed the birds? She's also the one who has brought in the plastic feeders. Melissa's job as logistics manager helps her haul in whatever her heart desires.

"Sentimental fool," Bill mumbles, but his fingers play with a small, soft sachet in his pocket. Sugary electrolyte gel to keep him from getting light-headed in the scorching sun. He brings the pouch to his mouth and rips it open with his teeth. When he nears the bird feeder, the hummingbird whizzes away. Bill squeezes out the liquid, spreading it around the perch of the bright red feeder. Then he steps back to wait.

"One hippopotamus. Two hippopotamus."

It surprises him how badly he wants the bird to return and find the sweet treasure.

"Seven hippopotamus. Eight hippopotamus. Nine hippopotamus."

That's all he can give the little sucker. Melissa might be foolish enough to waste her pouches of sugar on feeding the wildlife instead of saving her CCs until her chip gets fixed, but not Bill. He's smarter than that. Sugar is one of the most valuable products on the black market.

Does anyone else in the house spend money so carelessly? Would they use their CCs to purchase sugar, just to waste it on hummingbird feed? Definitely not the programmer, Jack. He hardly leaves his room. And when he does, everyone else is asleep or in the middle of night shift patrol.

The same goes for the rest of them: Abby, Arturo, Jada, and Radley. They all have titles, responsibilities, deadlines. The mansion seems to work like any traditional corporation. But not much about how their jobs work together in the company makes sense to Bill. And their employer is not one to elaborate. Guard, Head of IT, Administrative Assistant, Technician, Gardener; for the first two years, Bill must have seen his coworkers just a handful of times. Nowadays, he meets them once a week due to his duties as the mansion's CEO. He still has a hard time understanding why a mansion needs a CEO and not just a manager, but he does understand that there is plenty going on in this company that he doesn't know anything about. No one at the mansion seems to be willing to talk about their part in the business. And whenever Bill asks his boss about it, he waves his hand and says, "Don't you worry about it, son. You just keep the ball rolling."

Bill has asked Micky what he knows about Texas's business several times, but he doesn't know much, given that his job as the Executive Assistant for Facilitation doesn't require much information from the head of the corporation. He's the "errand boy," as Maria the maintenance woman calls him. Micky pouts and leaves the room every time Maria barks this nickname out.

Maria is more than just a maintenance woman. She manages the night shifts as well. Just like Earl, she doesn't have a problem with it, though she never brags about her prey, either. If the cold-blooded woman ever sleeps, Bill doesn't know when or where. Her bedroom is upstairs next to Bill's, but he's never witnessed Maria tucking in for the night. She's always on the go. Unlike most of them, she's granted passage in and out of the mansion whenever her heart desires. Where does she go? Bill's too afraid to ask. Or maybe he's too scared to hear the answer.

"Twenty-three hippo—"

The hummingbird appears out of nowhere. It hovers right at the red feeder and sinks its thirsty beak into the electrolyte gel. Bill can't stop a satisfied smile from spreading across his face.

Hover, drink, repeat. Bill stares at the bird. His coffee is getting colder by the minute, but it doesn't matter. It's already eighty degrees outside. Hot beverages and heat waves don't go well together. Just like his city-boy ego has had a hard time getting used to the country-living. "It'll get easier," he had told himself in the beginning. "You'll get used to it." But as the years keep rolling by, doubt fills his mind. City of California is, in many ways, just as corrupt as City of Finland, where Bill witnessed Kaarina escape the Chip-Center and run for her life only a month ago.

But it's still not the same. He feels bad for those working and living in City of Finland, spending their days pedaling like hamsters on a wheel. The standard of living is nothing like it is in City of California. Not even for those who have redeemed their spot in the AR-reality.

But above all, one thing separates the two cities from one another; Texas isn't exactly a mastermind, not like Doctor Solomon. Maybe Bill could use him, get access to the green city—

"Hey, you! Yeah, you. With the bare feet and a death wish," Micky hollers from the balcony above the porch. Bill closes his eyes, suddenly too tired to hear more jokes about his uncharacteristic mission. CEO or not, Bill hates patrolling. It's his weak point and everyone at the mansion knows it. An image of brown and bloody curls flashes beneath his closed eyelids.

His eyes water. He needs to distract his mind. Bill looks for the bird, listens for the whistling of its wings. But all he hears are Micky's words above him.

"You planning to take care of the invader with a coffee cup and your overgrown toenails?"

Bill rolls his eyes. "Who do you think I am, John Wick? And look who's talking, Micky. Bitch, please. I'm an assassin compared to your wimpy ass."

Micky gives him a small chuckle for the classic movie reference, and says, "You forgot this, silly."

A black backpack lands next to Bill's feet. Through the partly open zipper, the muzzle of a Glock peeks out.

"Are you trying to get me killed, you numb-nut?"

"Now, why would I do that?"

Bill picks up the bag, tempted to toss it back at Micky's smirking face. But he's always been terrible at throwing. Just as he's a lousy shot. "I don't know. To climb up through the ranks? To get a king-size bed?" He knows Micky would never. He cares too much.

"Relax, beau. It's a Glock. It has an internal safety. Three, actually. Earl told me it won't go off until you aim and shoot."

"Lucky me."

Micky leans against the railing, a happy grin on his face. "And you're hardly the boss around here, loverboy. We all know it's Maria who calls the shots."

Bill opens his mouth to object but then changes his mind. Micky's right. Maria always seems to know what to do. The best line of action, the smartest solution. Man, it annoys Bill, her being such a know-it-all.

"And why would I need a king-size bed when I already get to sleep in yours?"

He gives Micky the finger but can't help smiling. This place, this life, it would have gnawed a way bigger hole into his tormented mind if it wasn't for Micky. Bill throws the backpack over his shoulder. With one big gulp, he finishes his coffee. He places the mug next to an ashtray made from an old clay flowerpot.

He makes a beeline to the wire fence and slips through the hole in the metal net. Before he disappears into the rows of orange trees, he hears an amused voice join Micky's on the balcony.

"I'll bet you twenty CCs the only thing he'll shoot is a rattlesnake or his own feet."

Bill starts his walk through the plantation and mumbles to himself.

"We'll see about that, you blood-sucking vampire woman."

The trailer's white paint has yellowed from standing under the scorching sun for years. It's tucked between two avocado trees at the farthest corner of the premises. Here, a section of the fencing is missing, giving anyone easy passage into the farm. A dirt road wide enough for a truck and a trailer zigzags down the mountain's side. Below the road, a dried-out stream collects bones, broken or burned debris, old guns, and sometimes corpses.

Bill has been meaning to ask Maria why she doesn't just fix the collapsed fencing, no matter what Earl thinks of it. But he can't bring himself to mutter the question. Maria would just give him one of her black-and-white answers. One of her "it is what it is" statements. The way she's untouched by their ravished world sends shivers down Bill's spine. That's a side of

Maria she doesn't bother hiding, but Bill chooses to avoid contact with it.

A few months back, the trespassers stopped turning up once a week. These days, it's more like every two weeks between them. Maybe the word has gone out. Perhaps there are not many survivors left in what used to be the state of California. Whatever the reason, it took a while before the night shifts turned from a full-time job into a part-time gig.

Bill stares at the stained trailer on its ill-gotten premises, tucked away among the avocados. If only these people would stay where they're better off: among the wolves and coyotes. A persistent pressure at the back of his head alerts him. It's Kaarina, tapping him. Bill shakes his head, forgetting the trailer and the trespassing scavenger in it.

All that time, a full night of waiting at the balcony. And she's checking in *now*?

"Not the best time, Kay-Kay. No need for you to see this shit-show," he mumbles to himself, refusing to open the connection between him and his distant Unchipped friend.

Suddenly, the trailer door flies open. It flaps against the chipped yellow paint, its frame partly unhinged.

Startled, Bill ducks behind the closest avocado tree and tries not to move so he won't draw attention to himself.

Two young kids—a boy and a girl—run beside the trailer, giggling, chasing each other around. Neither of them looks old enough to walk, let alone sprint around. But then again, Bill knows nothing about kids. These ones are dressed in ripped, dirty-gray shorts and T-shirts. Their squeals and giggles sound foreign in Bill's ears–like they've landed from a spaceship above the farm. They might as well have.

Kids? Living and breathing outside the Children's-Center?

A man jumps out of the trailer, hissing something in Spanish. Bill can't distinguish the words. And even if he could, he wouldn't understand them. As he has a dozen times after moving to the mansion, Bill swears to himself that he'll use his leisure time to learn a second language. If only to understand the jokes in Spanish Micky makes at his expense. But then again, what's the use? Everyone speaks English back in the city.

A dark-skinned woman, lean but well-muscled, peeks out and then emerges from the trailer. "Inside. Now." She hangs out of the trailer's doorway, wildly gesturing for the man and the kids to follow her back inside. "Just because we're no longer in the valley doesn't mean we're safe. Get, get." Suddenly she pauses in her efforts. Frozen, listening. She hops down from the trailer and takes a few steps toward where Bill hides behind one of the lush fruit trees.

"Alejandro, did something move over there?"

Quickly, Bill pulls his head in and wraps his arms around the backpack. *Shit, shit, shit, shit.* The pressure in his head grows. It's almost too much for him to bear. Blocking the telepathic connection is not easy—it's starting to wear him out. But he can't have Kaarina seeing him on this mission. Shooting at people. Women. Freaking *kids*.

The man jabbers in Spanish. Bill hears the woman jump back up into the trailer and then down again. The sound of someone racking a shotgun echoes in the air. Bill's not sure which one of them is holding the gun; he hasn't seen either carrying one.

"No, Alejandro. I'm sure. Something moved behind the branches over there."

Dry grass rustles under her steps. Bill's now sure it's the woman who holds the gun. The man hasn't moved. He's stayed still by the trailer door, speaking long sentences in a language Bill is now dying to understand.

"Only rabid coyotes are out this time of day. If that's the case, I need to put it out of its misery."

The man argues with her.

"Zip it, Alejandro. Just let me go check." Her steps move closer to Bill's hiding place.

A freaking family. Who the hell brings kids into this nightmare of a world? he thinks to himself.

Carefully, Bill reaches for the Glock 22 inside the backpack. He fingers the trigger, hoping there'll be a safety on his weapon. Anything that'd slow him down and make him second guess his decision to take another life. Butchery shouldn't be an easy task. He had planned to talk to them, ask them to move on. Not shoot them.

The woman creeps closer. Bill can almost smell the gunpowder of an uncleaned shotgun.

This bitch is crazy enough to have kids. Which means she's crazy enough to shoot me.

Kaarina has stopped tapping him. The pressure disappearing makes Bill dizzy. For a terrifying moment, he thinks he might pass out. His body would then fall limp, exposing his position behind the avocados. His bare feet would point skyward while the woman would put an end to his contemporary clusterfuck of a life.

The careful footsteps stop on the other side of the tree, only six feet away from Bill. He'll never have enough time to turn and aim. He's a terrible shot: he wouldn't even hit the trailer from here. The scavenger mother would end him before he got the gun's safety turned off.

A sudden movement down the tree line startles Bill. A scream frozen on his lips, he turns around on his knees and aims at the woman. But the woman has also turned, her back now away from Bill. She aims her gun at a rabbit running down the small path between the avocado trees.

She shoots once. Twice.

Bill moves back behind the tree and closes his eyes.

The woman mumbles in the distance, but it seems like she's whispering straight into Bill's ear. She's walking away, back to her family. "Sneaky little shit . . ." A question from the trailer prompts the woman to sigh and call back.

"I know that, Alejandro. But rabbit stew would be a nice change from avocado burritos and rice. Don't you think?"

Her boots thump against the trailer's threshold. Bill lets the Glock fall back into the bag. Arms shaking, he allows the back of his hands to rest against the rough, dry grass.

The rows of avocado trees spin wildly around him. He breathes deeply to calm his mind, like Micky does while practicing Ashtanga yoga in the mansion's spacious hallways.

Body gives in. Mind follows.

Bill lets go of his failed mission. Of his near-death experience. This cursed place and the horrifying twist his life has taken since he drove through the farm's creaky metal gates two years ago. He lets his body go limp and his mind run free.

"What the hell, Bill? Why did you block me? Bill?"

But he's already passed out. Too exhausted to answer Kaarina's questions.

"And how's the Yeti? His brute ass getting on your nerves?"

Avoiding sharp rocks on the farm's small dirt roads, Bill makes his way toward the guard's shed. Inside, he'll find Earl. Lost in another tale of the Second World War, Putin Junior's biography, or some other historic moment Bill wouldn't have heard of.

"He's alright. Less of a creep now. I told him his so-called charm is more rape-y than anything else."

Bill scoffs but swallows his thoughts on the rugged outcast traveling with his distant friend. He doesn't trust the Yeti. Or anyone else that Kaarina travels with. The Chip-Headquarters must be the sickest, most manipulative place on the planet. Kaarina would be better off alone than traveling with the bunch of underdogs that used to live there.

"Hey, Bill? You do remember that I can read your mind, right? Though I'm impressed by your newly found self-censorship, you seem to have some severe anger issues to deal with. You know this, right?"

"I have anger issues? Ha! I am the most Zen brother left on this rotting planet." Bill's happy to be talking with Kaarina again. After the darkness he's started to feel lately, it's like coming back home or hugging an old friend, whenever they have these conversations. He wishes it wasn't just inside his head. That Kaarina could be here, and not just to entertain him, but to be safe.

"You should come here. Join me at the mansion."

"And let Earl report me in a nanosecond? No thanks. The green city may be fancier than City of Finland, but I'm pretty sure the stasis capsules are the same, no matter where they're located."

"I don't know. Maybe we could come up with a plan to actually live in the city but stay neutral. Like, not engage with the Happiness-Program?"

"I don't even know what to say to that. Except, have you taken your pills today?"

"I'm sick as shit of this isolation. What if these Chipped fuckers aren't all as corrupt as the hag in the white coat? Texas probably doesn't even know who Doctor Solomon is. Maybe we could turn him."

"And then what? Just sit back and enjoy the tall buildings and self-driving limousines?"

"Sure. Why not? And if they find us out, we'll be ready. We'll come up with a plan so great even Solomon can't see it coming."

"A takeover?" Kaarina pauses for a moment. *"This doesn't sound like you, Bill. Has Texas gotten under your skin? Should I be worried?"*

"Just worry about your own pale-ass skin, Kay. Nothing's gotten to me. Or, if anything, it's this crappy mansion and the morbid people I have to live with. I'm forty-one years old, Kay. I'm too fucking old to have a roommate."

"You mean roommates."

"Oh, go pound sand, Kay. Whatever. Just saying that having a CS-key and a place in the city would give us more power. And after a while, we wouldn't need Texas or any of the other assholes. We could start something on our own. We could start a revolution, Kay! We just need a way in."

"Oh, so you're going undercover now? You? Who can't lie to save your life?"

Bill doesn't reply. He thinks of the CS-key Texas has promised him. The opportunities it would bring.

"Why not stay in the mansion?" Kaarina continues with her relentless questions. *"You have everything you need. More than you need. And still, all you do is bitch and complain."*

"Yeah, well. I have my reasons. It's not all cheesecake and parties around here, Kay."

"Oh, really? What happened? One of your roommates stole your margarita mix, and you've been sober for half a day? Such a tough world you live in."

Bill quickly blocks their connection as images flash through his mind.

Blood splattered on the walls of the round wooden pen.

Long, wavy, brown hair turned into a muddy mess as the puddle of blood grows around a lifeless face.

He forces his mind to block out the traumatizing scene. Instead, he tries to come up with questions for Kaarina. Turn the conversation back to her escape from the head of the Happiness-Program. Bill opens the connection, hoping Kaarina hasn't noticed him blocking her again.

"So tell me more about this place you're heading to? Where are you going after your big-ass abduction mission is done and over with?"

It takes Kaarina a few seconds to reply. Bill's in luck: the Unchipped woman's been occupied with something else instead of Bill's mental block. *"Sorry, what? And it's not an abduction. We're just going over to find Niina's daughter. As soon as we have the CCs to travel."*

"After that, Kay. I don't care about some teenage dirtbag stuck in a home. I want to hear what happens next? You'll braid your Viking beards and live happily ever after . . . where?"

Kaarina turns silent. She focuses on her reality but doesn't block Bill from seeing her thoughts. Images of greenhouses, windmills, and natural waterfalls fill her mind. Gardens, horses, plantations, and small wooden houses fill a small and sunny village. On the meandering paths, people walk in pairs and groups, chitchatting, laughing. They're all dressed in mixed colors. No one wears overalls or augmented reality glasses.

A wonderland.

Did she make it up?

"What the hell is this place? Did you see it in an AR-trailer or something? Why don't you throw some unicorns in there while you're at it."

Kaarina hesitates and is about to reply when something or someone grabs her attention.

"Got to go, Bill. We'll chat soon. I promise."

"But you haven't told me how you're planning to travel about. Are you going to swim around the Atlantic or what?" Bill stops by the rose bushes that separate the riding arena from the mansion's driveway and Earl's gloomy shed. "Kaarina?"

It takes a while for her to reply. While waiting, Bill watches a man's pale hand reach for Kaarina's winter glove. The hand belongs to the Chipped mop-top. The same one that helped Kaarina escape the Chip-Center. Such a shit-show, this unlikely group of people.

"Go work on your anger issues, Bill. I'll tell you about the plan later."

The old man leans his face against his hands. Elbows tuck into a table made of old storage boxes. He's oblivious to the outside world. Just the book in front of him and his solitude. That's all Earl seems to ask from this life. That, and killing migrants.

Before Bill has a chance to knock on the door of the guard shed, the old man spins around. Only a split second and Bill stares down the barrel of a forty-five. Hands lifted in the air, Bill drops the backpack by his feet. "Jesus, Earl. It's just me. Didn't mean to sneak up on you."

With a low grunt, the old man with a slightly hunched back puts the gun down next to his book. He then reaches for a bag of tobacco and a package of cigarette paper. While he works on his cigarette, Bill fights the urge to ask if Earl would roll him one too. But as ridiculous as it seems, Bill doesn't trust the man enough to consume anything that has passed through his hands.

Bill stands taller, widens his chest. He feels like a kitten in front of a lion. "It's your night shift tonight, right?"

Another grunt. A puff of smoke.

"I was wondering if I could switch shifts with you? I can go tonight if you do my Saturday."

Earl lifts his feet up onto a storage box and leans back on his creaky office chair. The stuffing puffs out through multiple tears in the leather liner. "You and Micky got a hot date or something?"

Bill's too fixated on the trailer family to be annoyed by Earl's boorish question. The loitering scavengers must go. But the thought of Earl getting rid of them gives Bill anxiety beyond belief. He wouldn't slaughter a child. Two of them.

Would he?

Bill forces a grin. "Yeah, going to see Cher at Planet Hollywood."

"With wigs and high heels on?"

"That's the way we roll."

This fucking bigot, he thinks.

Earl finishes the tobacco with two long puffs. He tosses the butt on the floor and stomps on it with his army boot. Bill can't help but think how much he resembles the Yeti that Kaarina travels with. Earl's like an older version of the stern, roguish Finnish man. A deadlier version.

"Sure, I'll trade shifts with you. As long as you promise not to share any dirty details of your queer-fest."

After a courteous nod, Bill turns around to leave. Has Earl noticed how shaken up he is? Is he suspicious of Bill's uncharacteristic request?

"Hold on one second, party-boy."

Bill freezes on his spot but doesn't turn around to look at Earl. The nervousness lingering on his face would confirm whatever suspicions have arisen in the hoary guard's bald head. Bill waits for him to continue.

The office chair creaks when Earl leans forward.

"Is it true that Cher was really a dude?"

The mansion door closes behind him. The house seems quiet, though anything else would be alarming. Most of the tenants work behind closed bedroom doors. After two years of living together, there are still people in the house that Bill has barely exchanged more than a handful of words with.

The kitchen light is on. As Bill walks in, he finds Micky and Maria sharing a slice of cheesecake. Unlike the rest of the mansion's tenants, these two seem to seek out each other's company. Maybe it's because they've lived up here the longest. They sit by the kitchen island, both working on their forks to shove as much cake as possible in their mouths before it disappears from the glass pan Micky has baked it in.

Maria licks her fork and spots Bill standing in the doorway. "Hey, Billy-boy. How did it go?"

Micky looks up and raises his eyebrows. These two would have a field day if they ever learned about Bill hiding behind an avocado tree while his life was saved by a wild rabbit.

"All done and dealt with," he says, but the lie makes his voice shaky and weak. He blinks rapidly while he forces himself not to lower his gaze. If he did, they'd know he's lying. He needs to change the subject before Maria asks another question about his sudden interest in patrolling.

Bill walks to the fridge and peeks in. The shelf with his name holds two oranges and a bottle of ketchup. "Anything to eat around here?"

Micky abandons his fork on the table. Only crumbs of the cheesecake remain. He walks by Bill and disappears into the mansion's hallway. The hallway's pantry door beeps twice. Cups and bowls clink while Micky rummages around in the closet.

Maria collects the two forks and the empty pan from the counter and places them in one of the kitchen sinks. While running water into the tub, she lowers her voice and asks, "You didn't kill him, did you? The invader? You just scared him away."

This know-it-all vampire. Why does she have to see through him so easily?

All he can do is blink and stare. The new lie freezes on his lips. Usually, he'd be better at this. He'd have no problem coming up with white lies—or even outrageous ones. But seeing kids, a *family* out there, hiding and barely surviving . . . it nudged him over a mental ledge he was already having a hard time balancing on.

It doesn't help that he's out of his meds.

Maria turns off the faucet. She leans to grab a bowl and a spoon from one of the endless white kitchen cabinets. After placing the dinnerware on the kitchen island, she nods at Bill, gesturing him to sit down on one of the barstools.

A moment later, Micky arrives with three cans: chicken noodle soup, peas and corn, and a loaf of bread. He empties the noodles and the vegetables into the bowl and nods toward the microwave. "Should I heat it up for you as well?"

Astonished by his roommates' helpfulness and generosity, Bill shakes his head for a no. He's been careful not to ask for any favors. Owing people is not on his to-do list. These days, only three things remain on that list: One. Save up all the CCs he can. Two. Get his flawed chip fixed. Three. Move back into the city.

He starts to spoon up the cold soup.

Micky crosses his arms and gives Maria a look. When the woman shrugs a shoulder and focuses on peeling an orange, Micky starts with the questions. "So what happened out there today? A night shift, first thing in the morning? Care to elaborate?"

The sight of two kids running around the sun-bleached yellow trailer lingers in Bill's mind. The thought of Earl or Maria shooting one of them—*any* of them—makes his stomach turn. It makes him more tired than he remembers ever being in his life. He's just bought twenty-four hours for them by switching shifts with Earl. The thought of the old guard killing an innocent child seems too absurd for it really to happen. But something tells Bill he shouldn't count on that.

He lets his spoon rest against the bowl and reaches for the canned bread. Eyes blinking uncontrollably, he says, "I wanted to walk in broad daylight. Micky told me the rattlesnakes are everywhere now. Easier to spot those fuckers before dark."

Micky scoffs, crosses his arms, and looks at Maria. When the woman ignores him and picks another orange to peel, Micky moves his burning gaze back toward Bill. "Bull. Shit."

Bill shoves a chunk of bread in his mouth and gestures that Micky will need to wait for him to elaborate. Buying time won't do him much good. How is he to lie about a plan that he doesn't have? Should he warn the family so they can flee the premises? It's a known fact that all scavengers are feral. Out of control. No matter how much he wants to warn them, Bill doesn't want to get shot for a day's good deed. But then again . . . the family hadn't seemed feral at all.

"You let them go, didn't you?" Micky says, spreading his hands.

"And why would I do that? If Texas found out that I let a scavenger walk free, I'd be as fucked as a pornstar on a Tuesday."

Maria gets up and collects Bill's empty bowl and sets it to soak in the sink. Seeing her do such an ordinary task gives Bill the chills. A killing machine—that's what Maria is. How can she also be a real person? Someone who feeds her comrades and keeps the kitchen clean.

Micky relaxes his hands and walks over. He squeezes Bill's shoulder. "It's fine. We know how hard it was for you to . . . how difficult your first—"

Shaking Micky's hand off his shoulder, Bill quickly stands up. The bar stool falls behind him.

"Can you two just get off my ass? There was no one there, okay? The trailer was gone, vanished. How am I supposed to kill them all if they don't exist?"

Maria and Micky stand side by side with their arms crossed, their gazes drilling into Bill's blinking eyes. Micky cocks his head. "*All* of them? You mean there was more than one of them? In a single trailer?"

Shit. Shit. Shit. Is this day ever going to end? Bill's tantrum quickly dies, replaced with severe fatigue. His shoulders slump forward. He picks the chair up from the floor, sits down, and holds his head between his hands.

With one long stride, Micky's back by his side. "Hey, Bill, we get it. That's fine, it's all good. You're obviously not thinking straight. So he was gone before you got to the trailer. So what? One in, one out. Let's just forget about it."

A nod is all Bill manages. At least he made through his early morning patrol without killing anyone.

Brown hair.

A pool of dark red blood.

A scavenger. A hungry human being.

A bullet in her brain.

A gray, numbing sensation seems to come over him. It pulls him under murky waters, haunting him, tormenting. Sooner rather than later, it'll force him to visit the green city. To fill his prescription.

As he turns and heads toward the spiral staircase, Maria hollers after him. "You need anything, Bill?"

He stops but doesn't turn around to look at her. Why is she being nice? Bill is sure she's hoping for him to kill himself. Just so she can take his position as the mansion's CEO. Why else would Maria take an interest in Bill's needs?

"Actually, Maria, I do. Could you ask Melissa to take me to the city and back tomorrow?"

Bill doesn't have to turn around to know that Maria's frowning. But he knows she won't ask questions. She's never been the nosy kind.

"I'll do you one better. I'll drive you there myself."

CHAPTER 2
CITY OF CALIFORNIA

The black SUV glides down the mountain road and then to the valley: a small town that separates the mansion from the green city. Maria swerves to dodge a body in a blood puddle, rotting in the middle of the street along with other things that used to matter.

Disturbed by their surroundings, Bill mumbles, "How do people drive in this fucking mess?"

"They don't."

"What?"

"Nobody drives much anymore. Not outside the city."

Bill scoffs and tries to relax in his seat. "I guess you're right. Not much traffic around these days."

The SUV's front tire rolls over another bump on the road: could have been a brick from the broken-down strip mall. Could have been an arm or a leg. Bill curses under his breath.

"They could clean this place up a bit."

"Who's that?" Maria asks.

"What do you mean who? The people, woman. The people of the streets. What else do they have to do? Got nothing but time."

Maria gives him a look that Bill can't read. Judgment? Disapproval? Her eyes fix on the road, and her lips press into a thin line. They continue toward the glowing green city in silence.

An eerie feeling of someone watching him makes Bill twist uncomfortably in the passenger seat. The bodies don't bother him as much as they did in the beginning. Not after two years of the sound of machine guns and people screaming. They're safe up on the mountain but not isolated from the horror of The Great Affliction. These days most of the Unchipped die of hunger. But violent death is not a thing of the past, either.

Bill knocks on the tinted window next to him. "You sure this can opener is bulletproof?"

"Yes." Maria glances at him and shrugs a shoulder. "That's what Texas says. And why would he lie about it?"

"Because he's a murderous, sick fuck, that's why." Bill waits for Maria to deny it. To stand up for their employer. When she doesn't, Bill continues. "Maybe the car has hidden cameras. What if his fat white ass is sitting in his gaming chair, right now, betting CCs on how far we get before someone turns us into some scavenger's supper?"

"The guy's loaded. Having a bulletproof vehicle for his employees to use isn't that far-fetched, don't you think?"

Against his usual habits, Bill doesn't share one of his conspiracy theories. He doesn't remind Maria that Texas could be just another scam artist among a thousand more. Not as bad as Doctor Solomon and her crew, but not as smart either. Maybe his idea of taking over Texas's place in the city is not as far-fetched as Kaarina makes it sound? He's smarter, more patient, and in ways more resourceful than Texas will ever be. He could play the man easily.

The mansion was supposed to be temporary. A safe haven while Bill decided where to live, and what he was to become. But as of late, the walls have started to close in. The same apathetic faces, sneaking around each other, avoiding any social interaction. Without Micky and Maria, Bill would have been a complete hermit for two years now. The same white walls, the same idiotic product orders, the same scenery of a sleeping mountainside—it was enough to drive him mad. Even the fruit now tastes like cardboard.

It seems everyone else refuses to see the mansion for what it is; just another prison. Just another way to control them, to keep them locked up until the city is ready to deal with those it left outside to rot.

But he's too tired to debate. To make Maria see the façade they live in. The fake-ass titles and jobs. The patrolling. It's all so meaningless. A parking spot for the Unchipped: damaged goods that don't fit anywhere at the moment but still too valuable to someone to be tossed away.

He's jaded. Run-down. This time the depression has crushed him in record-breaking time.

Bill stares into space and thinks of his friend on the other side of the world. Has Kaarina noticed the difference in him? The lack of witty comments and sharp assertions? Maybe she hasn't. She's too busy chasing unicorns and promised lands. The way she now focuses less on Bill and more on the hobos she travels with annoys Bill more than he'd like to admit. She knows the old Bill, the one who is okay with living in the mansion, day-drinking and cracking jokes. Maybe Kaarina sees him as one of the AR-products people wear in the city: When you take off the AR-glasses, they don't exist.

The SUV stops by the city's electric fence line. Maria slides the driver's side window open and taps on the electronic pad by the main gate. Soon, a guard dressed in green overalls appears from the nearby building.

"Your host?"

"Mister Dennis Jenkins."

"How many guests in the vehicle?"

"Two."

"Chipped or Unchipped?"

"The latter. Both of us."

The guard puts a pair of government-issued AR-glasses on. They blink and reflect a slight neon-green light. The sight of them starts a familiar, throbbing tickle at the back of Bill's head. *Great, I'm not even in yet, and the city's attacking me,* he thinks.

After a minute of waiting, the solid metal gates open. Maria drives into the city. Bill taps his chest pocket for sunglasses. Not for the early morning light, but the green glow that now assaults him from all around.

Maria nods at the glove compartment. "There should be extras in there. Grab me a pair too."

Bill fishes out two pairs of oversized sunglasses and hands the pair with small diamonds to Maria. She looks like a rock star or a Chipped influencer. A VIP. Invincible. Immortal.

But Bill knows the light hurts Maria just as much as it hurts him. Still, this Unchipped woman doesn't show any sign of discomfort. The glasses do help, but they don't help that much.

Maria drives into the Chip-Center's parking lot. They keep going until the lights go dim and turn into normal blue light. It's the same light they have at the farm and everywhere outside the AR-driven city. She stops the car, using two parking spots instead of one. Bill frowns at her asshole parking job. Maybe she's just provoking him, hoping to get him to snap out of it.

Bill clears his throat and takes off the sunglasses. "Need any painkillers? Allergy meds?"

Maria pats on her pockets, gesturing she's all covered. "Just be fast. And don't let them sweet-talk you into moving into the Chip-Center. The mansion's far from perfect, but it beats that institutional hell-hole any day."

Bill huffs at her words. Maria's right, as usual. The Unchipped living in the Chip-Center have it way worse than Maria and Bill do; they are like prisoners of their own damaged minds. Captured, controlled, and inevitably growing crazier by the day.

"Wait here?"

Maria spreads her hands: where else would she go? Which is hardly true. Maria's always on the go. Doing ...*something*. Bill's dumbfounded that the workhorse took a morning off. Just to help him out.

He gets out of the car, slams the door. With determined steps, he walks into a building where they once changed Bill's future of feasts and festivals into a dreadful game of moral compromises and lying in wait.

"When was your last manic episode? How long did it last?"

Bill has refused to lie on the leather couch. With his hands crossed behind his back, he hovers by a full bookshelf at the far wall of Doctor Baldwin's office. He knows that the hundreds of books written by Freud, Kempler, Fulani, and Perel are only for show. Nobody reads them anymore, not in this form. All the books are now either in audio format or turned into chip-movies, played through the CS.

"I wouldn't call them manic episodes, per se."

"What then?"

Bill turns to glance at the doctor. "Huh?"

"What would you call them if not manic episodes?"

Bill turns back to stare at the hardcovers. He pulls out a book so thick he needs two hands to flip it and read the back. An image of Earl, caressing his gun and reading his hardcovers, stops Bill from investigating the book further. He pretends to finish reading the description and slides the book back into its designated slot.

"I guess those are just times when I feel more upbeat. Energetic."

The doctor taps something into his electric pad. His fingers hesitate, stop, and hover until they continue again. He's struggling. Bill being in the room prevents the doctor from using the CS devices. Bill wonders what would happen if he handed the man a piece of paper and a pen.

"Any risky behavior? Any grandiose delusions?"

Bill laughs briefly. "Like that I'm Jesus, or a sexy immortal god of thunder, or something funky like that?" Bill blows air through his lips. "Please."

"And risky behavior?"

Bill shrugs and turns to face the doctor. "I walk around the farm with no shoes on. Tons of rattlesnakes out there. Does that count?"

Doctor Baldwin taps the tablet but doesn't answer Bill's question. "And how do you sleep?"

"Like a fucking baby."

The doctor looks at him for a second longer but doesn't comment on his cursing. Frowning in frustration, he taps on the tablet in silence for a full minute. Bill wonders if he's more annoyed at having to treat an Unchipped person or because of the old-fashioned technology.

Aren't those two things one and the same?

The doctor finally puts down the tablet, gets up, and walks to his desk. From the drawer, he pulls out three bottles of pills, way smaller than what Bill had been hoping for. He wonders if the medicine is 3D printed or as ancient as the electronic tablet tucked under Baldwin's arm.

"Same as before: Aripiprazole for manic episodes—"

"Upbeat times, you mean," Bill says.

The doctor shakes his head slightly but agrees. "Yes, Aripiprazole, for your *upbeatness*. And Lamotrigine for depression. Start with two today and continue until it's time to switch."

Bill wants to ask if the good doctor finds it morally wrong that old medicine like this is being used to treat the Unchipped. The expiration dates are worn from each bottle and package Bill has ever gotten from him. But he doesn't care enough to start a debate. The pills work, so whatever.

Instead of questioning Baldwin's morals, he asks, "What's the third bottle?"

The doctor drops all three bottles into a green fabric bag, walks over, and hands the bag to Bill.

"Tylenol. For your meeting with Mister Jenkins."

Bill walks up to Maria in the shady parking lot and tells her he'll continue on foot. Texas doesn't live too far away from the Unchipped hospital's parking lot.

"You're sure you can handle that?"

"What kind of a weak-ass quitter you think I am? It's not that long of a walk. A mile, maybe less."

"It's less than half a mile. But filled with billboards and holograms. You'll be screaming in agony before you make it to the skyscrapers."

Bill wants to tell Maria that she's wrong. That the excruciating pain and nausea won't bother him. But he'd be lying. And she'd see right through him like she always does.

Unsure why, Bill wants to spare Maria from the physical pain the city will cause her if she joins Bill where Dennis Jenkins lives. Sitting and waiting in the middle of the glowing AR-city will give her a headache. The headache of the century.

Bill shakes the fabric bag he carries. Pills rattle in their bottles. "These babies could knock out two Earls, maybe three. I'll be fine. I'll ask him to keep it short. Unless you're dying for a long-overdue Texas meeting yourself?"

Maria's glare is meant to be contemptuous, but her relief shines through. None of the mansion's tenants are big fans of their employer. But Jenkins pays them well. Lets them live on his luxury farm. Far enough from trouble, in a place where they're safe and separated from the violence and restlessness. Free from subjugation behind the Chip-Center's institutional walls.

Glowing green billboards and digital signs of all sizes rise around Bill. He can't see the holograms but feels them vibrating in the air. Careful not to step on the neon-green tiles that meander around the buildings, Bill makes his way into the heart of the city.

Cool, fresh air breathes out from everything around him. It's not too warm, not too cold either. The perfect weather. In the distance, three enormous Vertical Farming-Centers throw their shadows on the Children's-Center and endless rows of skyscrapers.

Self-driving limousines pass him at their robotic pace. Nobody walks in the city. Not on the tiles or beside them. People don't need to leave their apartments to go to work. They can plug themselves into the CS in the comfort of their luxury apartments. They only travel for pleasure. For entertainment like game shows and fights. Even at the theaters, everyone gets a booth of their own.

Complete, ultimate privacy.

Three identical self-driving limousines pass by. Behind the tinted windows, the Chipped stare at the stranger in a strange land.

"Keep staring, dick-face. I'm really one of you, you know. Or do I look like a hungry-ass hobo to you?"

He wants to hate them, the privileged assholes driving by. Despise their luxury vehicles and apartments and lives. He wants to believe that City of California has absolutely nothing to offer him. That what Texas calls a paradise is just a corrupt can of worms. That the only purpose this place has is to turn people into vegetables and store them inside stasis capsules.

He wants to spit on the green tiles as well as the shiny black limos sliding by. He wants to be above it: the scam. The make-believe. Blinking promises and shining products that can only be seen through truth-bending glasses. Consumer goods that his own hands have helped design. Millions of CC s invested in fake lives. Fake furniture, fake outfits, jewelry, pets, AR-companions . . .

But he envies them. The fuck-faces in their shiny limos. Texas, running the show from his high tower.

What if he was to change it all? Turn this place into something new completely. A utopia. Art, science, schools, nature—all the things that once were available for anyone. He just needs to find a way in—

"You're still on that, Bill? Becoming a mole and taking over the green city?"

Bill's smile is instant. The nagging pain that has moved from the back of his head to his temples eases off when he hears Kaarina's calm voice inside his head.

"Look at you, Kay-Kay. Finally, ditching the tramps and joining my company. I didn't think you'd make it."

"And miss a meeting with Texas? Doesn't sound like something I'd do. What pranks are we going to pull on that sucker this time?"

"I was thinking about telling him that the earth has turned flat overnight. But you need to leave the city to see it."

Kaarina laughs briefly. *"Genius. He will never know."*

A comfortable silence falls between them. Bill walks down the main street, cursing the doctor for giving him such small bottles. He'll surely need to revisit the city in a couple of months.

"What are those pills for anyway? You've never told me why you take them."

Damn it. He wishes she didn't keep bringing that up. It's not that he doesn't trust her. He just fears Kaarina would look at him differently—or worse, pity him—if he was to tell her he's bipolar.

"You told me to work on my anger issues, didn't you?"

"Yeah? And since when have you ever taken advice from me?"

"Touché, girl."

There's a pause while Kaarina ponders her words, but Bill can feel them coming. Bill wishes the woman would just leave it be. No such luck.

"Bill?"

"Yes, ding-dong?"

"You do know that I've lived inside your head for years now?"

Bill walks on and doesn't reply.

"I know you struggle. I've been there through your good times, and I've been there through the bad. I know this situation is getting to you. Believe me, it's not easy for anybody. I make jokes about margaritas and cheesecake, but I know things are a mess for you too."

"And?"

"Well, it's just that . . . Just that I . . . well . . . "

"Jesus on a bike. Just spit it out already."

"I know you're bipolar, Bill. And it's okay that you didn't want to tell me. I can respect that."

Bill laughs bitterly. "So you can respect that I'm not willing to talk about my mental health with you, yet here you are, talking about it?"

"I know, I know. I just . . . "

"Good lord, girl!"

"I just want you to know that I'm here for you, okay? You have good things going for you. It's not all bad. So please stop thinking that the city is the answer here."

Bill stiffens. "I'm not."

"Bill, like I said, I live inside your head. I know about you being bipolar, just as I know about that night when you—"

"Yes, yes, yes! The city is a scam. The chip is the devil. Texas is a shady-ass con artist, and you can read minds. I get it, Kay. I was the one who taught you that, if you'll recall. So just drop it, okay? I don't have time for your bullshit. Because, look," Bill waves his hand at the building in front of him, "I have arrived at my motherfucking destination. So you can either stick around and keep your thoughts to yourself, or go play with that mopheaded boy-toy of yours."

When Kaarina doesn't reply, Bill buzzes a number by the locked front door. Only a few seconds and a familiar Texas accent echoes through the speaker. "Bill? Is that you, my friend?"

"Yes, sir. In flesh and blood."

"Fantastic. Hold on. Let me hit the lights."

They stand and wait in silence—Bill and Kaarina— until the green lights die off. Window by window, the building turns into a gray shadow in the middle of a glimmering city. The light reflecting through the see-through front door turns warm yellow. The front door buzzes open.

Bill climbs the fire stairs to the fifth floor. There he takes a breather, grateful for the tinted windows that reduce the glare of the city's neon-green lights. For the next hour or so, this dull gray building will stand out in the ocean of blinking lights, solar tiles, and fast-paced hologram advertisements. Good thing Texas owns the whole building. Otherwise, the tenants might riot and remove Bill, carry him back to the street. If they could agree to step outside their privacy bubbles, that is.

He continues his climb. One stair after another, he gets closer to a man he'd rather not have in his life. But then again, Texas is the very reason Bill is not locked up, monitored, poked, and prodded in that hellhole of a Chip-Center. Not every Unchipped is as lucky.

And the Chip-Center aside, he could be one of the corpses in the valley. The ones that Maria drives over without blinking an eye.

On the tenth floor, he stops again. Five more to go. His eyes lust over the metal computerized locks on the apartment doors. Each of the heavy plates has a small, green blinking light, stating that it's in use. Each of the locks claims the apartment as somebody's property. The key to the lock is integrated into the small computer: the tenant's handprint, combined with their brain chip. No other hand could ever open the lock. No visitor—invited or not—can enter the tenant's bubble of privacy. Not even Texas.

"Beats having a dozen roommates," Bill mumbles to himself. He wishes he had one of these apartments, secured by his very own CS-key. It would give him the peace and quiet he needs to come up with a plan. A plan that would change not just his future, but that of everyone in the city. He'd be a different kind of a leader. The good kind. Powerful, but loved.

Somewhere above, a metal door opens with a *whoosh*. "Bill? You coming or what?"

He finishes climbing the stairs and walks into Dennis Jenkins' apartment.

Bill sits down in an uncomfortably low couch chair by a fake bonfire. He looks around the balcony through his sunglasses. Though his wristwatch tells him it's only two p.m., the fire and the gray day make the scenery seem like nighttime. The eerie green light prompts him to close his eyes and turn his back on the city.

Inside the apartment, Texas's living room opens empty and hollow. Without AR-glasses, the furniture is limited to a couple of chairs, coffee tables, and a wooden cabinet at the back of the room. Bill wonders if Dennis sleeps in an actual bed. Or maybe he has some sort of a new digital wonder product to catch his z's on.

"Whiskey okay?"

Texas hands Bill a lowball glass with brown liquid inside. Bill takes a sip and doesn't know where to set the glass. There is no table in front of the seats. He sets it down next to his loafers. His host gives him an amused look but doesn't say anything.

After turning and sitting down on a sturdy gaming chair placed between the balcony railing and the fire,

Texas smiles and watches Bill through the AR-glasses. The blinking green lights make Bill wince.

Bill's employer's eyebrows rise. "Oh, these things bothering you? Here . . . I don't need them." With a quick hand movement, Texas takes the glasses off. "Is that better, my friend?"

Bill gives him an awkward smile and reaches for the whiskey. Doctor Baldwin told him not to drink with his medication, but Bill hasn't taken the first pill yet. The alcohol might help with his headache.

Something catches Texas' attention. He stares at the whiskey glass next to Bill's loafers. "I'll be damned. Was that not a real sculpture by the fire? You put your glass right next to it without commenting on it."

"Yeah no, I don't see anything here. What does it represent?"

"Huh?"

"What kind of a sculpture is it?"

Texas thinks for a second, then waves Bill off. His laughter rumbles and echoes around them. "Never mind about that, son. About time I took these babies off, I guess."

After he tosses the AR-glasses onto an empty couch chair next to Bill, Texas rotates his chair toward the city that opens in front of them.

"Beautiful, ain't it? Not sure what people mean when they say it's gray and boring without the glasses.

One can find beauty in all sorts of things. Even in real life. Don't you think?"

Whiskey burning his throat, Bill forces himself to grunt agreeably. He doesn't want to look at the gloomy but disturbingly bright city. Instead, he reaches for the whiskey and finishes it with a single gulp. This gets Texas's attention.

"Are you out of booze at the farm? You seem awfully thirsty."

Bill places the glass back down and grins. The liquid burns his chest and stomach on its way down. "There must be a dozen boxes left in the pantry. Trust me, we're all set. And I say this despite knowing Earl's drinking habits."

Rumbling laughter shakes the leather chair underneath the overweight man. He's dressed in a black shirt and pants, not in green overalls like most people in the city. Maybe it's because he's the head of the city. Or maybe it's just the guards and Chip-Center employees like Doctor Baldwin who wear the official city clothing. The only people that can still be seen in the private, digital city.

The Chipped do see each other, but only inside the virtual gatherings—in simulation rooms. Their CS-avatars wear the latest digital outfits, hair, and body shapes, preferably something that no one else has discovered and purchased yet. In a city that holds nearly four million people in it, this must be a challenging task.

The Chipped in City of California seem to have dedicated their lives to finding the next trendy thing. Bill is familiar with their consumer habits. He designs the AR-goods they keep buying and hoarding. And they bring him more CCs than Bill can count. Once he's back in the city, he'll be able to buy anything. He could even afford to travel, though airfare is by far the most expensive thing out there.

The whiskey goes straight to Bill's head. Though it makes him dizzy, he welcomes the numbing sensation that eases the pounding headache.

"Not a big drinker, huh?"

Bill shakes his head carefully. "My meds don't go well with this stuff."

"Ah, yes. Bipolar, right?"

Bill can sense Kaarina focusing more closely on the other side of the world.

"Of sorts. It's not as bad as the doctor thinks. I manage without drugs most of the time."

"Well, with a working chip, that wouldn't be a problem at all. The Happiness-Program is known to solve all mental health issues in a matter of a few quick months. Just like those who were once deaf can now hear, and those who were blind can now see. You'd feel as good as new."

"Why is he throwing salt in your open wounds, Bill?"

"I know it's been a long wait. It's been two years since I hired you. A year since I made you the CEO and promised you your very own CS-key and a spot in the sun. You probably thought it'd take months, not years? I did too, to be honest. To show you my appreciation, I've doubled your pay and given you a well-deserved bonus. It's already transferred to your CC account."

"Whoopie. How are you supposed to use all this money when you're not even living in the city? Dumbass."

Texas gets up and walks to Bill. When he gestures toward the empty glass, Bill hands it to him.

"Let's get you another one then. It's a rare occasion. You here, drinking. No need to half-ass it."

As Texas walks back inside to fill two empty whiskey glasses, Bill closes his eyes. He waits for Kaarina to tell him how Texas is no better than Doctor Solomon. How City of California is just as rotten as City of Finland. But all he hears is stubborn silence.

A glass half-empty appears in front of Bill; Texas hands it to Bill directly.

"Listen, son. I have some news to share with you. As you know, I've been pleased with your work at the farm . . ."

"What work? Your Poodle-gators? Please."

Since when has Kaarina been this focused on offering commentary?

"But it's time for you to move back in. To where you belong."

Texas hands over a blue paper file. Surprised to see a cardboard folder, not an electric pad, Bill takes the file and opens it. Personal information and medical records of a man Bill has never met or heard of fill the thick stack of pages. At the bottom of the pile are multiple CT scan pictures and medical charts.

"What's all this?"

Texas sits back down on his gaming chair and crosses his hands behind his head. When he smiles, Bill spots a pattern of deep-red lines from the AR-glasses. Does he sleep with those things on too?

"Mister Thomas S. Williams. First Californian Unchipped whose chip was removed, repaired, and reinstalled. He got his CS-key last week and now lives two stories below me."

"Those look fake to me, Bill. If they could fix the Unchipped, everyone would know about it. Not just some egotistical low-life in City of California."

Numbers, charts, and words teem in front of Bill's eyes. Bill knows Kaarina's right, but the thought of living in the city with a working chip and all his needs provided for makes his throat constrict with longing.

"Bill, it's fake—"

I know, I know. A part of the scam. Just shut up, would you? I can't tap you and have a conversation at the same time.

"You, my friend, are next. Congratulations, son. We're bringing you home."

Bill sets the papers down in front of him. He gets up and walks to the balcony railing. Up in the sky, a thick blanket of clouds blocks all sunshine. The morbid gloominess reminds him of some other place, but he can't think of where he's seen this before.

If he lets them cut into his brain, the city lights won't hurt his eyes. If Texas's story about a fixed Unchipped man is true, that is. But it isn't. They just need more test subjects, more data on the damaged chips.

"Would I get to stay here even before the procedure?"

"What's that, son?"

"If I say yes, would I get to move in to wait for my chip to be fixed? Would you turn off a part of the building for me?"

Then, he'd lack for nothing. No more corpses, no gunshots echoing from the valley. No more night shift. No more two-room living quarters. He'll have an enormous apartment of his own. A balcony with a pool. A fireplace. AR-glasses. Invisible sculptures. He'd live as happy as a hummingbird in a pool of electrolytes, while coming up with a master plan to take over Texas's operation.

"You could move in tomorrow, if you so desire. I'll have a floor with no green light. Why not? There's plenty to go around. There is just one thing we need from you first."

"Here it comes. You can stop drawing out your crown and throne."

Bill hears Texas get up from the gaming chair. Heavy footsteps approach. The older bald man joins him by the railing.

"Nothing major, just a favor my colleague from City of Finland recently requested. She's traveling to City of California, actually. Should be here later today."

Kaarina's rising panic clicks across Bill's skull.

"Up there, at the North Pole, there has been an outbreak of sorts. Chaos and disorder. Which is unheard of in City of Finland. People there are usually easily controlled and mellow. They do as they're told, and they get a safe, protected life for it. It's a win-win in every way."

Texas takes a sip of whiskey before continuing. "A lot of people have gone missing. This person—a young woman—leading them is known to be connected with a man who once helped her find a missing person here in City of California. Ring any bells, son?"

Shit.

"He's working with Laura Solomon. She's coming for us. You have to run, Bill."

"And what if it does?" Bill says to Texas, doing all he can to remain calm. "Ring a bell, I mean?"

"Then, I would like you to contact this girl. Ask her where she is. Once you have her location, come and see me. We'll get you moved in right away."

Shit, shit, shit. Bill stays quiet. Kaarina's heartbeat races in his ears.

"Unfortunately, your friend has stirred a pot that should never have even boiled. City of Finland is in chaos. An uprising was mentioned."

"I, um . . . " Bill starts, but Kaarina screaming in his head makes it impossible for him to answer Texas.

"That's bullshit! People are supposedly free to leave the city and the Happiness-Program whenever they want to. Laura said so herself. Twenty people joined me and moved away. Who cares?"

"Hundreds of Chipped individuals have gone missing, Bill. Some people now refuse to work in the Server-Center, asking for explanations that are way beyond their paygrade. Even the employees of the Pedal-Center and the Vertical Farming-Center are getting restless."

Bill can hear Kaarina hold her breath. He can hardly breathe himself. Not only is Texas familiar with Doctor Solomon's tyranny, but he *works* for her as well. Or with her. It doesn't matter that the man is a tad simple. Not if he has a genius like Solomon backing him up. Bill should walk away. Abandon his scheme and plans of hostile takeover. But his loafers are stuck on the balcony's solar tiles. His eyes are fixed on the AR-glasses, blinking on the couch chair.

"And what happens when they find her? Last time they tried to shove her in a capsule and turn her into a turnip. Why would I tell them where she is?"

"Because that's the right thing to do. Doctor Solomon believes people will calm down once the rebels return. They're doomed, anyway. How are they to travel? And where would they go?"

Texas rummages through his pockets and finds a small, green-glowing box. Soon he lights up a cigar that looks more like a space shuttle than a cancer roll.

"Besides, my friend. Are you sure that's what happened that day? She was hardly turning into a turnip. The girl ran before they were able to fix her chip. To turn her into one of the Chipped. That's all Laura wanted to do. Help her. It's not our fault the girl gave away her second chance to be integrated with the blue city. And for what? Some flimsy and ridiculous conspiracy theories."

"I'm going to kill this birdbrain! They were going to shut me down. Bill, you know this. You were there."

His heart racing in his chest, Bill turns and nods toward his whiskey glass by the fake fire. "I need to hit the head. That stuff goes right through me. Where's your bathroom?"

Bill walks toward the door Texas points out, all the way at the other side of his spacious home. He's too afraid to talk with Kaarina with Dennis in the same room. The man has no idea that Kaarina has heard every word of their conversation.

Bill gets to a metal door, presses a button to open it, walks in, and presses another button. The door whooshes shut.

"Bill, you were there. You know that Solomon is evil. It was you who told me to run in the first place for crying out loud."

I know, Kay. But let's think of our options here. Texas may work with Solomon, but maybe we can keep her out of this, Bill replies silently.

"How on earth would we pull that off? Bill, you're delusional. They work together. She's asked about me. We can outsmart Texas, maybe, but we can't outsmart Laura Solomon. There's no way."

Bill rubs the bridge of his nose. *But if we could just get them to fly you over. If you were here. Together we could—*

Kaarina's sputtering interrupts his words. It takes a while until she finds her words again. *"No, Bill. There's too much at stake. You can't fix this. You can't tell them where I am and assume it'll give you some kind of lever-age. You need to snap out of this fantasy, Bill, and you need to do it now!"*

Bill sits down on the toilet seat. He doesn't have much time.

What if I fly you over and we don't tell anyone?

"I'd have a minute and a half in the mansion and one of your zombie friends would call Texas to let him know I've arrived. No, Bill, I won't be any safer in City of California. If anything, you'd be better off here, where it's less violent."

But what if I had an apartment in the city?

"I wouldn't have a CS-key to it."

Yeah, but you'd live with me.

"I know, Bill. But I'd still be trapped."

I would make it work. We would make it work together.

"That's a fantasy, Bill. Not real life. You are not omnipotent. You're not even Chipped for fuck's sake!"

Yeah, but what if I was?

Kaarina shakes her head, huffing words Bill can't understand. *"Voi sinä hyväuskoinen imbesilli . . . "*

Kaarina, you know I don't speak Swedish. Can you switch back to English, please? I'm just saying that we should talk about—

"Don't 'just say'! How can you even suggest putting me at risk that way? And what about all these people that follow me? You want me to just abandon them?"

I just want to consider all the options we—

"Since when have I had options? This is you playing with my life. And for what? So you can get a luxury apartment and access to all-you-can-eat vegan buffets? Look at me, Bill. Take a real good look. I have two sets of clothes, shoes that give me blisters, and no place to call home. I'm on the run. Most days, we all go to bed hungry. And yet, I would never hand in another Unchipped. Never. No matter what they offered me."

You know I don't care about the stuff. I'm just saying that if we come up with a plan—

"And now, let's take a look at your life. Living in a mansion? Check. Eating cheesecake for breakfast? Check. Margaritas for supper? You bet. You have friends around you. You have a job. You're safe. Why isn't that enough, Bill? Why can't you be happy with what you've got? I know it's not perfect, but when compared to most of our lives, you're living the dream."

Flashing images of brown curls lying in a puddle of blood rush in. As quickly as possible, Bill blocks their connection before Kaarina can see what he sees. A girl who had been about the same age as Kaarina. A girl who did nothing wrong. Except finding herself in the wrong place at the wrong time. Just like Kaarina now.

A careful knock on the bathroom door startles Bill. "Did you fall in, son?"

"Be right out."

He forces his mind to block out night shifts, rifles, and dead girls. After taking down the mental barrier, he continues tapping Kaarina.

Listen, I'm sorry. You got me all wrong. I would never sell you out or risk your life. That's not what I was suggesting at all. I just know that I can do this, make a plan to beat Texas and use him to get us power in the city. A real change, Kay, that's what I'm after. And then . . . You and me . . . We could both live here in this city. I could hide you in my apartment. Nobody ever sees anybody around here anyway, and we'll turn off all the AR-bullshit. There'll be plenty of rooms for you to choose from. Hell, I'll give you the master bedroom. How about that?

Bill lifts his head from his hands and listens. "Kaarina?" He stands up and bumps his head with his fists. *Shit, shit, shit, shit, shit.*

"Son? I got another whiskey waiting here with your name on it. Come drink before it gets too late. Didn't you say you had a ride coming to pick you up?"

Bill's head falls back into his hands. *Maria.*

He stumbles and hits the faucet button. A stream of water sprays the front of his pants. He storms out of the bathroom.

"Here." Texas hands him a familiar-looking lock. "A promise of what's to come. I asked them to program it so that it'll work even before we fix your chip. Just come back tomorrow with your belongings, give us the girl's location, and claim whatever unlocked apartment you want. Plenty to choose from."

Bill grabs the CS-key from Texas's hand. "Thanks. Gotta run." He storms out the door and onto the staircase before Texas has time to reply.

It's not only Maria waiting for him that has slipped his mind. He's also forgotten about a certain loitering family in a stained yellow trailer.

CHAPTER 3
2 YEARS EARLIER

City of California's Chip-Center, 2086

Two doctors stand by his hospital bed, reading a chart, comparing pictures. Bill guesses them to be brain scans, but his vision is still blurred after someone drilled a hole into his skull and installed a microchip into his cerebral cortex. The beds beside him are empty. Everyone else has already left or moved or died. Bill doesn't want to know which.

One of the doctors steps forward. In a monotonous voice, he says, "Thank you for your patience, William. My name is Doctor Baldwin, and I'm afraid I've got some bad news for you. The chipping procedure hasn't gone as planned. I'm here to help you cope with this unexpected turn of events."

"You're a shrink?"

"I'm a psychotherapist, specialized in chipping and Happiness-Program patients."

Though he's clearly talking to Bill, the doctor keeps his eyes on an electronic tablet and a patient chart he holds. For a minute, Bill wonders why he needs both, but then quickly decides he doesn't really care to know. The doctor finally looks up and notices Bill eyeballing his equipment.

"You're wondering why I'm not using the Chip-System devices? It's because the glasses alone are enough to make some chip-patients feel extremely nauseated."

"I definitely feel nauseated. And I definitely don't give a fuck about your glasses."

Bill feels hungry, out of place, groggy, and disoriented. Despite what they promised him, he isn't about to jump into his brand-new self-driving limousine with tinted windows. He's not on his way to one of the skyscrapers, about to rest in his spacious apartment with a pool and a green view. All this should have happened in a matter of hours, right after the chipping operation.

Yet here he lies. Still in hospital clothing. Achy. Starving. All that was promised is suddenly denied: the limo, the apartment, the augmented reality. His brand-new, carefree life in the green city.

Now, the only thing new is a throbbing hole in his head.

Bill spreads his hands and then points at his partly shaved head. "So put me back under. Finish what you started."

"I'm afraid it's not that simple. We'll need to run some tests, get a good look inside to see what could be causing the issue."

Bill is losing his patience, the annoyance and disappointment buzzing through his mind. "None of this was discussed before the procedure. Why wasn't I warned that this could happen?"

"It's extremely rare that this happens. I am sorry this happened to you. But the good news is that you're not the only one whose brain failed to accept the chip."

"How the hell is that good news?"

"Well, you'll have company here at the Chip-Center. You may not have a view, and the city is known to make people like you ill. But you'll have access to all the shows and services. Just not through the CS."

"What the fuck is a Chip-Center? You mean the hospital?"

"You're in the Chip-Center right now. It's part of the hospital. We have the whole lower level reserved for patients such as yourself. The system is new, and it's still in beta, but we're learning more each day. The global research team is exceptional."

"There's a group of failures like me living in the hospital basement?"

"I wouldn't call them failures."

"What would you call them?"

"Excuse me?"

"If not failures, what would you call these unlucky bastards, watching TV while you suck their blood and probe their brain?"

The other doctor turns and leaves the room. Maybe the conversation has started to bore him. Baldwin clears his throat and looks up from the charts.

"We call them Unchipped."

The smudge-guard makes his pinky numb. Since seven a.m., Bill has been cooped up in his bedroom. The drawing tablet and a bag of mixed nuts are his only companions. In a way, he does have company— another Unchipped individual. Hiding in the middle of the woods on the other side of the world. Hiding in his head.

When they first met a week earlier, Kaarina and Bill quickly decided not to freak out because of their inexplicable connection. They agreed to focus on coping with their new lives as outcasts instead. Most of the time, they avoid each other. It's a rare occasion when one taps the other.

A careful knock on the door gets a grunt out of Bill. His uninvited visitor is most likely Micky. Maybe Maria. He hardly sees anyone else in the mansion.

His eyes linger on the piece he's worked on for the last hour: an oversized digital scarf with silhouettes of cats on a silky surface. Flustered, he sets down the electric pen. "Come in!" he yells and then mumbles, "If you must."

The dark woman walks in without a sound. Maria's catlike way of moving has fascinated him—and creeped him out—since day one. Today is day twenty-five, and Bill still hasn't gotten used to the hair-raising way she moves. He turns his back to her and stares at the order list in front of him. Two more to go and the order will be filled.

Maria's muscular body leans against the studio's doorframe. "Micky asked me to tell you he's back from the grocery run."

"Mmm."

"In case you want to stop starving yourself."

"I have nuts."

"A grown-ass man will surely die on that diet sooner than later."

"Aha."

"Wouldn't want to drag your corpse out of that chair. I could ask Earl, but he'll be too busy reading and shooting rats by the barnyard."

Bill turns around and glares at the woman. He wonders if "rats" is a metaphor for something other than actual rodents.

It's clear to Bill that Maria is testing his limits. But he finds her way too intimidating to snap at or argue with. So he lets her keep pushing his buttons, hoping he won't one day explode and strangle the woman. Not that he'd be able to: Maria's stronger than the margaritas Bill has for breakfast.

Bill's the newbie. The only reason Maria shows him at least some respect must be their mutual boss, Dennis Jenkins.

They all call him "Texas" because of his thick southern accent. Ever since Bill got hired to live and work in the mansion, Texas has taken a special interest in him. What for? They all have their suspicions.

Without a sound, Maria walks over. She peeks over Bill's shoulder. "Whatcha graphic designing, graphic designer?"

Maria's elbow brushes against Bill. Though he's afraid of this woman, even a slight touch like this sends a warm sensation through his body. When's the last time his skin touched someone else's?

Bill lifts the drawing tablet for Maria to get a better view of his work. "An order from the city. Texas wants it returned in three days."

"Today's day two?"

"Day one. I still have a pair of glowing high heels and a parrot-rat to draw. Pays three hundred chip-credits, this crap. Per item."

He points at the tablet with the cat silhouette scarf, shining in all rainbow colors. "I would love to meet the twisted individual whose ideas I'm drawing. Just so I could punch them in the face. It's like polishing an endless pile of turds. Can you believe someone would want to buy this thing? To *wear* it?"

Bill lifts the drawing tablet a bit higher. "I don't care if it's digital or augmented or virtual or fucking magical. It's crap and a disgrace."

Maria shakes her head and chuckles. "Oh, Billy-boy. You don't need to understand it to draw it. Who cares what those assholes wear?"

"You do understand that one day you'll be one of those assholes, right? Strolling down the green tiles, wearing this bad boy?" His finger taps at the bright scarf.

Maria shrugs her shoulder and gives him a crooked smile. "We're here now. Not in the city. It is what it is."

"And it doesn't bother your Unchipped ass? The *what it is*?" Bill's afraid to hear her answer. But maybe he's wrong about her. After all, Maria's here, showing somewhat normal emotions. Like a living, feeling creature: a decent human being. Not a cold-blooded murderer who walks around the farm, shooting coyotes and rodents and people. Never blinking an eye.

Her hand brushes against her shaved head. "I think anyone who claims to be happy in this hellhole is full of it. Anyone who says they haven't at least dreamed about living in the city is lying. We were supposed to end up there, after all. We are the one percent."

"So you *don't* like it here? You hate your job, just like I do?"

Tell me you hate it. Despise it. That you'd rather die yourself than dispatch another scavenger.

Maria considers his words, then shrugs. "Meh. I don't mind my job. Fixing things has always been something I enjoy."

Bill squirms in his seat. "How about the . . . the *other* job?"

Maria raises her brows and stares at him. Then a crooked smile twists her unusual but striking face. "Should have known you meant the night shifts. I knew patrolling would bother you. I knew from the moment I found you and your duffel bags in the front hallway." Maria picks a piece of paper from Bill's work desk. It's a green diamond, shining with all the spectrum's colors. For any personal projects, he still chooses to draw on actual paper.

Maria places the paper back on the table. "Whether it makes me a monster or not, I don't really think about it. It's just the small print in my contract. Something I must do to survive. I don't think the morals and ethics we used to live by apply anymore. Not in this new reality we live in, not for anybody, whether you live in the city or outside of it. If we'd live in this new world by some outdated moral code, it would be like offering ourselves up for death."

Bill turns his gaze away so Maria won't see the agony her answer causes him. Why does it matter what she thinks? They aren't friends. They are barely colleagues. Why is it so crucial for Bill to see the good in this obviously twisted and ruined person?

"Your money's on me being a monster, I see." She chuckles a bit and continues. "Well, in that case. Yes, Bill. It bothers me. It makes me lose sleep. Their dead faces haunt me at night. I wake up screaming. I cry for those who once thought it'd be a good idea to break into someone else's premises and make a nest. It's torture, Bill, but guess what?"

Bill shakes his head and closes his eyes. Her sarcasm is only making things worse.

"It doesn't matter. None of it does. Whether you judge me or not. Whether you treat the night shifts as a part of your job or let them stigmatize you. Whether you consider the outsiders as scavengers or just unlucky people in a horrible situation. Whether you keep on being a pussy and crying yourself to sleep every night. Does. Not. Matter. The aftermath is still the same."

"Which is what? People dying because they stole an avocado? Parked their vehicle in the wrong place?"

Maria turns her back and walks back to the door. "Sure, that's part of it. But what's the biggest difference between them and you?"

Bill spreads his hands.

Maria taps the doorframe twice before she disappears into the dimly lit upstairs hallway. "You're still alive, Bill. They're not. Might as well enjoy it while it lasts."

One year. That's how long Bill was able to avoid patrolling. For a reason he never learned—though he had some ideas—whenever it was Bill's turn to do a night shift, Maria would come to him and say, "I got it. You go draw."

Later those nights, when a rifle or a handgun went off somewhere around the farm, he told himself it was just Earl shooting rabbits or rats by the barn.

One year, and then Micky finds him sitting by the front porch. Bill's enjoying his third cigarette of the night, but when Micky appears, a throbbing pain attacks Bill's temples. Something blinks in Micky's hands: a headset, AR-glasses. "It's for you. Texas."

Refusing to show Micky how much agony the glasses bring him, Bill puts them on. Micky and Maria seem to tolerate the pain so much better than he does. He watches a tacky trailer of a green-glowing city and its perfect tenants. A place with zero sickness, zero worries, zero violence. No hobos. No mass-shootings. No suicides. The city doesn't have night shifts. Nothing that dramatic would fit into a place that provides only good experiences. Pure happiness, which only a few are privileged enough to enjoy. Bill should be one of those few. It's just that his brain refuses the chip that'd make it all a reality.

The AR-glasses press against his face. They make smoking difficult. It's hard to see his own hand in the alternate reality. Bill tosses the butt into a vase down by the porch stairs. He should quit anyway.

"Bill! Good news, son!"

Texas is one of those people whose good news could just as well mean a gigantic comet hitting earth, destroying what's left of the nearly extinct population. Or it could mean a hefty raise for everyone in the mansion. It all depends on what it brings to Texas himself. What happens to the rest of them is beside the point.

"I've just got off the phone with my colleague in City of Finland. We're cooperating on a project that focuses on the failed chipping subjects, such as yourself. We're especially interested in a claim that you Unchipped folks are somehow connected, well, telepathically? Care to elaborate on this?"

Bill's hands twitch to take off the AR-glasses. The small, green lights, together with the flickering trailer movie, are making him sick to his stomach.

He forces his hands to leave the headset alone. "There's not much to tell. I woke up after the procedure and found someone living inside my head. I know others can do this too. Anyone with a broken chip in their brain can, as far as I know."

"All Unchipped are able to do this? So why is it that you alone are connected with one of these special friends?"

"I'm sure I'm not the only one. But people don't talk to people they know anymore. Let alone to strangers."

"And you found your trusting friend . . . how exactly?"

Bill contemplated how much he'd be willing to tell his employer about Kaarina. "We don't know. Just that our chipping procedure was on the same day. And both of us ended up Unchipped."

"Fascinating. Truly." Texas takes a break to suck on a cigar. "Well, got to tell you, my friend, you might need to find another way to connect with this special friend of yours. If what they say back in City of Finland is true, we'll be able to integrate you with the CS very soon."

Bill perks up in his seat. A herd of coyotes yaps somewhere nearby. Maria's out early, doing the rounds. No gunshots yet. Though the night is young.

"But listen. I know it must be frustrating to just sit and wait for your return to the city. Science and technology and all that crap is not exactly something I excel in, but lucky for us both, I do have friends in all kinds of high places. So, I know it's going to happen for you, the Happiness-Program, and the city. And it's going to happen sooner rather than later."

Bill picks up another cigarette and lights it despite not being able to see it very well. He inhales the smoke and holds it in until he feels like he is suffocating. Pain from the AR-glasses drills into his skull and face.

"While we wait to become neighbors, I would like to offer you a promotion. If you manage to fulfill a few simple requirements, I'll make you the new CEO of the mansion. I am not really into that job anymore. The scene in the valley is too disgusting for me to consider leaving the city."

"CEO? Can I still draw?"

"You can do whatever your heart wishes, my friend. Just look after the others. Make sure they do their jobs. This makes you single-handedly responsible for the premises as well."

Bill swallows the smoke. "You mean the night shifts?"

"Yes, the night shifts. But you don't have to do all of them, son. That's not what I mean. Actually, now that you're in charge, you don't need to do *any* of them. Unless you want to."

Who would voluntarily go out and shoot people?

"But I do need you to successfully do it once. Show the others how it's done. Put on a little show while you're at it. Show them you got balls."

"That's the requirement? For me to slaughter someone in front of the others?"

"Tonight. You need to do it now. Talk to Earl. Tell him you'll do his shift tonight. Tuesdays are his nights, yes?"

An image of a grumpy man holding onto a bottle of expensive whiskey and a brick of a book fills Bill's mind. It was the guard's night off, and against his usual habits, he had taken it. "I'm pretty sure he switched shifts with Maria."

"Fine, Maria then. That black cat is a machine. She keeps the farm cleared of scumbags and thieves like no one else. And she does it while fixing anything that's broken! That's why I made her Head of Maintenance. How does that old saying go, two birds and one stone, something like that?"

With shaky hands, Bill lights another cigarette while the previous one still hangs from his dry lips. Unsure whether it's the smoke, or the glasses, or

Texas that makes his stomach flip, he gags and bends far over.

He isn't a killer. Not in the slightest. That's why he's here and not in the valley. Graphic designer, lying low, but free from the institutions. That's the plan. Not liquidating people.

"Do this for me. Take over the farm, keep it clean, keep it organized. Do this, and as soon as we're able to fix a malfunctioning chip, you'll be the first one to move back into the city."

That night Bill meets with Earl. He had agreed to Texas's terms. One shift. One kill.

He had retched after his call with Texas ended.

Earl walks out of his guard shed just in time to see Bill folded over the rose bushes. "You had one of Micky's meat pies or something, rookie?" He walks over, holding a Glock 22 and a small pouch of bullets. "Climbing the ladder, then? Huh, Bat-Boy?" He hands over the gun and the bullets. "You know how to use one of these?"

"I do."

He doesn't.

"It has an internal safety, or three of them. Point, aim, shoot. A monkey could do it."

"I said I know how to use it," Bill lies, blinking rapidly. If the old man knows he's lying, he doesn't show it. Fear, repulsion, and regret mix in Bill's stomach as he stares down the mansion's guard.

Earl stares back at him, a dull expression fixed on his gray face. Bill nods and turns around. He starts toward the rows of orange trees, silhouetted against the setting sun. The scent of rotting fruit makes his stomach flip again. When he's sure he's far enough for Earl not to see him, Bill hurries to one of the metal horse stalls and dry-heaves into a broken bucket.

Six hours. That's all he'll need to suffer through. Maybe just walk around and stay out of harm's way. The trespassers usually break into the farm from the east side. Maybe if he just stays near the front gates? Maybe then he will miss all potential intruders?

But he knows it wouldn't count.

Crickets fill the heavy night air with continuous chirping. The coyotes have traveled down east of the farm, teaming up somewhere by the dried-out stream and the rickety fencing. There they prepare to hunt down their next feast: a rabbit, a skunk, maybe a small deer.

It's dark. So dark that Bill has a hard time seeing the gun's silhouette in his hands. He turns one of the plastic buckets upside down and sits.

He'll just stay here. Wait it out. The horse stables have always been his favorite place at the farm.

Possibly because none of his roommates ever visit them. Except for Earl shooting rats. Those nights, Bill stays as far away from the abandoned barn as possible.

A sudden movement in the dark catches his eye. The motion sensor clicks. Floods the barnyard with bright blue light. Behind the round pen, a shadow presses against the wooden wall.

Bill jumps up and grips the gun with both hands. *Please be a raccoon. Please be a raccoon . . .*

A lock of brown hair peeks out from behind the round wall. The girl—an intruder—tries to figure out whether she's alone in the barnyard. She hasn't spotted Bill, standing in the shadows by the open barn aisle. Stolen fruit rolls out from the bag the girl had been carrying. One of the oranges rolls across the yard and into the barn aisle. Bill stops it with the tip of his loafer.

He presses his back against the stall door and tries to steady the gun in his shaking hands. Will the intruder be smart enough to run back to the hole in the fence? Back where she came from?

Bill needs to get away from this hellhole. Get back in the city, the only remaining nook of civilization and humanity. But to do so, he'll first need to prove his worth. But why is his worth being measured by this horrible metric? Would a humane and civilized society really demand something like this? Or is this part of the new moral code that Maria talks about? If it is, Bill still doesn't get it. Any of it.

The motion sensor clicks again, killing off the blue light. He is practically blinded now in the sudden dark, his vision barred by the red halo left behind by the floodlights. He can't help a long exhale that makes him sound like a leaking balloon.

In the distance, one of the mansion's balcony lights turns on. Bill presses against the stall door, trying to recognize the silhouette leaning against the bedroom's balcony railing. His balcony railing. But he's too far away to see who is staring at the spot where he and the intruder are hiding. Whoever supervises him has chosen a prime location to witness what's happening in the barnyard.

But nothing has happened. Nothing will happen. The brown-haired girl will pick up the bag and sneak back to a path leading to the orange trees, then the avocados. Then, another track that'll take her back to the valley. One of the crazies there can then put an end to her starvation. But not Bill. Not today.

Two silhouettes now stand on the balcony. There they spy on Bill and this sickening job interview, which could cost him what's left of his damaged mind. Barely breathing, Bill slides down against the stall's metal door, hoping the intruder will be wise and do the same.

Hide. Stay hidden.

He stares at the round pen, then back at the mansion. A new shadow walks on the balcony. It takes something off its back and places the object against the railing.

A sniper rifle.

Of course. How has he not figured it out until now? One of the shadows will be Earl or Maria. Both of them will have what it takes to finish the night shift on Bill's behalf. They'll be the new CEO and first to move back into the city. This job interview is not just for Bill. He just has the first shot at it.

The brown-haired girl will end up dead. Whether Bill punks out or not.

The thought makes him dizzy. Would Maria gun him down too? Earl surely would. He'd probably enjoy it. They'd AR-call Texas announcing Bill as collateral damage. His apartment with a view, his new life, will then be handed over to whoever takes the shot and finishes this night shift.

A click in the dark makes Bill jump back up. The blue light flickers back on.

No. No, no, no, no, no.

Near the pen, the girl stands, shaking, torn sneakers landing carefully against the ground. She moves to pick up the bag, collecting the runaway fruit. A thick cloud of brown hair floats around her picturesque face, making her look magical and out of place. Her fragile jawline and small button nose seem familiar to Bill. Has he met this girl somewhere before?

His feet heave, and the gun trembles in his hands. Bill steps out into the blue light.

The girl looks up, gasps for air. Her whole body frozen, she lets the fruit and the bag fall back onto the ground. She lifts her hands. "*Por favor . . .*"

They haven't met before. This intruder doesn't speak English—unlike the girl she reminds him of. The one that lives inside Bill's head. His only friend.

The cracking sound of a bullet splits the air. A small chip of wood flies off the round pen's wooden wall. The girl kneels, arms covering her head.

Bill looks over his shoulder. At the balcony, one of the silhouettes holds the sniper rifle; its barrel still pointed at them. It's impossible to tell who it is shooting at them, but there are only two people who could make that shot: Earl or Maria. Either way, the bullet missing its target is no accident.

It was a warning shot.

Bill takes a step closer to the intruder. He lifts his Glock and aims. "Run. You need to run. Now," he hisses. The steady flow of adrenaline in his ears muffles her response. But even if Bill could hear the words, he wouldn't understand them.

Bill keeps his gun aimed at her. "Please, just run . . . *Va . . . vamos, la señora?*"

Another shot slices through the air. It lands closer to the girl's head. She screams and folds herself over, presses her tiny body against the round wooden wall. She's too terrified to run away.

Bill knows two things. One: The shooter is Maria. Earl isn't known for giving third chances. Two: The next bullet won't miss.

Bill takes a step back. With shaking hands, he aims the Glock at the shivering, crying girl pressed against splintered wood. When Bill's hopeless cursing reaches her ears, she starts screaming. She sounds like an animal, run over by a car. A thing in pain. A suffering creature too weak for this sickening world they must live in. Bill's scream mixes with hers.

The Glock goes off.

Its soul-ruining, stigmatizing sound echoes in the night.

CHAPTER 4

BETWEEN THE AVOCADO TREES

"What the hell happened, Billy-boy? Did you pound a bottle of whiskey and piss your pants?" Maria drives the black SUV through the quiet streets in the valley.

Bill sits with his knees folded against his chest on the passenger seat. He waits for Maria to make a mocking comment about it: how he looks like a teenager, returning early from summer camp because he's too homesick for his mother.

He buries his face against his knees. "I fucked up, Maria. I fucked up big time."

He can nearly hear the woman frown.

The sound of three gunshots echoes through the valley, along with sharp clinking sounds as the bullets hit their targets. Bill sinks into his seat, breathing rapidly. Briefly, Maria places her hand on Bill's shoulder. "They're shooting at glass bottles. It's all good. Relax." Her uncharacteristic kindness startles Bill more than the gunfire.

"That's cute, Maria," he says. "Like those poor assholes would have extra ammo to shoot bottles for fun."

Maria waves him off. "Whatever. Believe me, don't believe me. Just ignore it."

The green fabric bag shakes in his hands as Bill reaches for the pill bottles. After checking the label, he pops one of the containers open and takes two pills. Maria reaches behind her seat. Despite the awkward way her arm bends, the woman doesn't struggle when she hands Bill a gallon of spring water.

"Does your fuck-up have something to do with the Vikings?"

Bill takes a long gulp of water, some of it spilling on his already-rinsed pants. "You mean the Finns?"

"Who else? What did Texas want? Is that chick you're tapping in trouble?"

Twisting uncomfortably in his seat, Bill curses the way Maria reads him so effortlessly.

"That's exactly what Texas wanted. Kaarina. And of course she had to be there to hear it all, and of course her dramatic ass completely overreacted when I didn't immediately jump down Texas's throat and burn down the building. The stubborn doofus she is, she wouldn't let me explain myself at all. And then I had to block her, so she wouldn't learn about me shooting..." Bill's voice cracks and he needs to pause for a breath. After clearing his throat he continues. "She just can't know about that night. Kaarina freaks out if it's just a deer dying . . . or a rabbit or a freaking raccoon. She just wouldn't get it."

"So you shot someone, yes. We've all had to compromise our beliefs and morals to survive. If she doesn't get it, she doesn't get it. So be it. It doesn't make you a bad person."

"If me shooting someone doesn't make me a bad person, I don't know what the fuck does."

"New rules, new world. Like it, don't like it, doesn't matter. Now quit swimming in self-pity and just drop it."

Maria steps on the gas pedal. They've gotten to the lower part of the mountain road that leads to the mansion. From here, Bill knows that Maria can remember the potholes by heart.

Bill squeezes the fabric bag like it's a blanket and he's a baby trying to fall back to sleep. Fighting the temptation to suck his thumb, Bill asks, "Why didn't you take the shot that night? I know you missed her on purpose. If you hadn't, you'd be the highest on Texas's list. The first to move back into the city."

Maria keeps her gaze on the meandering road. The sun would soon set behind the mountains.

"Who says I want to live in the city?"

"I just assumed—"

"Never assume, Billy-boy. It'll get you killed one day."

"I don't need to assume that living outside the city turns you into a murderous scumbag. I've seen what living out here does to the human psyche. They've all lost it, these poor assholes. And can you blame them? Living in fear like that, fighting for cans of moldy food. I feel for them, Maria. I really fucking do. But it doesn't mean that I want to become one of them. The city is a nasty place run by nasty-ass people, but it's the only place where a person can lead a somewhat civil life these days. Out here, you're done. Turned into an animal. Trust me, Maria."

Maria doesn't reply. Her lips press into a thin line, her eyes fixed on the rough road.

A section of the dried-out stream comes into view. They're almost at the intersection before the mansion when Maria suddenly takes a hard left. Her unexpected U-turn takes them back toward the valley. Bill holds onto the oh-shit-handle.

"What the actual fuck, Maria? Where are you going? We're almost home."

She doesn't answer. Just reaches for the gallon of water on Bill's lap. With one hand, she brings it up to her lips while with the other hand she holds the wheel. Bill had needed both hands to lift the damn thing.

"Don't worry, we're still going home. We're just taking the scenic route."

A rusty pink van stands out against the high metal fencing. Bill stares at it, his fingers still wrapped around the handle above the passenger seat. Maria's U-turn took them across the valley, up a snaking mountain road, and onto an old vineyard that has been out of business and people for years now.

Or so Bill thought.

The sun sends its last beams down to the vineyard before it sets behind the mountainside. The low hum of a generator reaches his ears. Glowing red, tiny chili pepper light bulbs cast a warm light around a sitting area beside the van, where partly collapsed picnic tables and stained plastic chairs are strewn about. A delicious mix of smells enters through the SUV's air vents: spices, cooked fish, caramelized onions.

Bill's mouth pops open. Without turning to look at Maria, he stares at the pink van in awe. "I know this place. They used to offer wine tasting and had the best Mexican food in town. This place is still in *business*?"

Maria huffs half-heartedly, a knowing smile on her face. She parks the car where rows of dead twisted grapevines begin. The winery is dark and worn-down, except for the red, glowing sitting area in the middle of the twenty-acre winery.

"Why? You thought there were no other civilized communities out there? Just Texas playing house with the braindead? And our little cabin-fevered crew of ten? Bill, please."

That's exactly what he had assumed.

When Bill's eyes get used to the dim light, he's able to read the sign above the van.

MARISCOS Y TACOS

All he can do is stare. At the sight of civilization. At the slightly tilted van.

Inside the taco stand, a man moves back and forth. Steam rises from a plate of hot food he carries from point A to point B and then to C. His weathered hands pick taco fillings from plastic bowls, add flavor from spice shakers. The smell is to die for.

And isn't that exactly what's going to happen if Bill gets out of this bulletproof car? Has Maria completely lost her mind? But then again, the cook doesn't seem nervous or surprised to see visitors. What is this place?

Bill watches Maria place her gun on the dashboard. Without looking at Bill, she opens the door and gets out of the car. Smooth, catlike steps take Maria to the taco stand. The man cooking inside looks up and nods at her. After a minute, he sets a plate of steaming food on the serving window. Then he turns his back on Maria and starts working on a new dish.

Maria takes her plate and strolls to a picnic table with rusty nails and splintered wood sticking out. Somehow, she's able to sit down without damaging her ass. She picks up a soft-shell taco and takes a bite. Out of nowhere, three pit bulls trot over to the lonely diner. They sit down in a neat row next to her. Maria grins and reaches out to pet their heart-shaped heads.

She's been here before. Not just once or twice. She's a regular.

Bill reaches for the door handle and hesitates. Would Maria have brought him here, knowing someone could harm him? Stab him? *Kill* him? He steps out of the car and slams the door. Maria picks up another taco from her plate, never looking back at the car.

Bill walks to the serving window. The sound of his heart pulses in his ears. The radio is on, playing an old roots reggae song Bill distantly recognizes. The taco man sings along and swings his body to the rhythm. Bill fills his nose and lungs with the heavenly scent of Mexican food. When's the last time he had a taco? Two years ago? Three? Mouth watering, his heart stops beating wildly against his chest. He clears his throat.

The cook turns around and stops swaying his hips. His relaxed demeanor vanishes. His body turns rigid. Frowning, he investigates Bill from his bun to his soaked pants. Then his eyes flicker to Maria and back. "You with her, man?"

Bill fights the urge to fix his loosened bun. Instead, he corrects his posture, pushing out his chest to feel stronger, more confident. It doesn't work. He feels weak and vulnerable under the tall man's gaze.

"Yes . . . Yeah, I'm with Maria. Man."

The man's eyes measure Bill for a few seconds longer. Then, he shrugs and asks, "Beef or fish, man?"

Bill's eyes flicker to Maria and the dogs. "Fish is fine. Thanks."

The cook claps his hands together so loudly it startles not only Bill but two of the dogs as well. One of the pits doesn't notice. He has climbed up next to Maria, greedily picking up the small pieces of meat Maria places in front of his slobbery snout. He's dodged all the sharp edges pointing out of the wooden bench.

He's a regular too.

The metal plate clanks against the serving window's metal surface. Bill collects his fish tacos, mutters his thank-yous, and makes a beeline for Maria and the dogs. He circles the beasts to sit down at the opposite side of the table. The dogs keep staring at the dining woman.

Maria licks her fingers. Breaking some sort of a taco-eating world record—Bill is sure—she has finished the last of her five tacos. After carefully sitting down, Bill takes a bite of his unexpected choice of dinner. The heavenly taste forces him to close his eyes. He chews slowly, savoring the flavor. The divine food in his mouth feels ill-gotten. Like he doesn't deserve this kind of a treat.

His mouth full, Bill opens his eyes to look at Maria. "How do I pay him? I assume he doesn't have a CC account?"

Maria rolls her eyes. "Don't *assume* your pretty little head over it." She tears off a small stick from the damaged table and starts picking her teeth. "I'll take care of it."

In silence, Bill eats the rest of the tacos. The dogs are now lined up next to him, drool dripping from their sloppy mouths. Bill turns slightly on his seat to get away from their demanding stares. But when his eyes travel back to their soft, sorrowful eyes, he can't help but drop a few pieces of fish on the ground. By accident, of course.

As Bill picks up the fifth and last taco, a man and a woman, both dressed in bleached, time-worn overalls, appear by the side of the van. Once they see Maria and Bill, they stop where they are. The woman leans in and says something to the man who then proceeds to the serving window. The cook greets the young man cheerfully, and Bill sees that this man, with his shaved head and gray-white overalls, is also a regular. The older woman brushes her fingers through a cloud of curly gray hair. With a deep sigh, she limps to the table and sits next to Maria, her slightly hunched back turned away from Bill.

"I thought we had an agreement."

"We did."

"No more noobs, Em."

"Won't happen again, Hawk. Promise."

Maria tosses her homemade toothpick on the ground. The dogs run to verify it's not a piece of food. "Bill's cool. And he'll pay double the CCs for our tacos. I'll make the transfer tonight."

Bill's eyes flicker from the gray-haired woman to Maria's relaxed figure. They're not carrying guns. None that he can see, anyway. Both of them have now turned their backs on Bill and are leaning against the table, elbows supporting their upper body weight.

The old woman shakes her head, smiling. "Since when do you hang out with white collars?"

"Since when do you feed the dogs instead of cooking them?"

Hawk's low chuckle relaxes Bill. These two know each other. They're, if not friends, then some kind of acquaintances. The woman elbows Maria in the ribcage. "Always good to see you, Em."

The young shaven-headed man makes his way over to the table. He carries a large metal tray filled with chips and guacamole, more fish tacos, and three burritos. Bill wonders if they're chicken burritos but doesn't want that to be his first question. He stays silent, knowing his expression matches that of the three begging dogs. Those five fish tacos were the best thing he's eaten for years, and Bill would definitely eat more.

The man, or boy—he can't be more than sixteen or seventeen years old—sets the tray on the table and sits down next to Bill. He eyeballs Bill and then gives Maria an amused look. "You down with moneybags now, Em?" he asks, reaching for a burrito. Once he takes a bite, Bill's mouth starts watering again.

Maria laughs a little and turns to face the table again. The old woman does the same.

"What's wrong with wealthy people, Marco? Not all successful people live in the city," Maria says, smiling.

Marco grins and shrugs. "I guess I always thought you were after the thugs and bad boys, like Hawk here."

The old woman picks up a corn chip and throws it at Marco. Amusement in her voice, she says, "Oh, what do you know, you little shit." Hawk reaches for another chip and dips it in the fresh guacamole. "Thugs were never my thing. I'm more of an emotionally unavailable, narcissist type of a gal."

Maria chuckles and turns her focus back to the dogs. The biggest hound, the same one that sat next to Maria stealing pieces of her meal, has stacked several sticks up by the table. Maria reaches for one and flings it toward the parked SUV. All three dogs take off running.

Bill's fingers twitch for the chips and guac. Is he allowed to eat from the tray? Are there more outsiders living at the winery? Are Hawk and Marco Unchipped or completely chipless? It's impossible to see the woman's skull through her wild bundle of hair. Bill moves his eyes to investigate Marco's shaved head. Like a mind reader, the boy catches on immediately.

"Looking for a scar, newbie?"

Everyone stops what they're doing. They all stare at Bill. He doesn't remember ever feeling this out of place. This . . . shy.

"I didn't mean to be nosey—"

Hawk's laughter interrupts his words. "That's okay. It's a valuable piece of information, in this day and age." She smiles at Bill and continues, "None of us have a chip. Never had one, never will. Before The Great Affliction, most of us were stay-at-home-moms. Plumbers and hairdressers. Sandwich artists, office workers . . . you know—regular people living our regular lives. We also lacked the good fortune of having family members or friends in high places. Not all gardeners can have rich and powerful parents like Em here," she says, again elbowing Maria playfully. Something dark shadows Maria's face, but only for a second. Regret? Shame?

"We were successful in life, but not in everyone's eyes. There are no reservations for us in the city, and there never were. We were always supposed to be left behind."

Scavengers? But they seem so . . . normal. Unhostile. Sophisticated. Maybe Texas could help them? Bill searches for Maria's eyes, but the woman is occupied, now playing tug-of-war with two of the dogs at the same time. Knowing Maria won't notice, Bill investigates her face. Maria has wealthy parents? Are they still around? In the city? He's never asked about her life before the mansion. And Maria has never volunteered to share what her life was like before.

"What's in the bag, moneybag?"

Like a reflex, Bill moves the green fabric bag away from Marco.

"And what happened to your pants?" Hawk asks, with a teasing tone in her voice. Bill looks down at his sprayed shorts. If the sun had been out, they would have dried a long time ago.

"A rogue faucet. What happened to your leg?"

Marco glances at Hawk quickly before he lowers his gaze. He focuses on nibbling at his burrito and staring at the table.

The old woman leans her elbows against the table. Clearly unbothered by his question, she investigates Bill's face for a good while before she answers. "An incident at the city gates. I tried to talk the guards into selling me a medicine we ran out of and desperately needed. But they weren't interested in doing business with underdogs."

A Chipped fired a gun at her? Inside the city limits? That can't be right.

"Did you shoot at them first?" Bill asks, immediately regretting his question. Another assumption.

All three around the table smile and scoff at the same time. At least Bill doesn't seem to have insulted the old woman. But he has to stop blurting out these assumptions before he does insult someone.

"Hawk doesn't own a gun, Bill. All weapons are stocked outside the winery. No weapons are permitted on the winery land. This is a safe haven for those who don't want to live in the city," Maria says. She wipes her hands together and finally meets Bill's gaze.

He's been wrong. About so many things.

"Is this where you come when you're not at the mansion?"

While he waits for an answer that never comes, Bill's eyes scan the dimly lit yard. "How many people live here?"

Hawk pulls a gray curl away from her face. Taking a handful of chips from the metal bowl on the tray, the old woman nudges it toward Bill. "More than me, Sly-Taco, Marco, and the three slobber-machines here? Of course, there's more of us."

"And the Chipped. Do they know you're here?"

"Not if you don't tell them. This is why we agreed with Em, here . . . "

"No newbies," the two women say at the exact same time. Maria lifts her legs on the seat and wraps her arms around her knees. "Like I said, it won't happen again. I just figured you could use some CCs before I can bring in more supplies."

Is this where Maria's food and supplies go? Every week, she fills the grocery list just like everyone else, but all Bill has ever seen her eat is the fruit she collects from the mansion's trees. She's feeding scavengers? Just to come back to the mansion and shoot them?

Hawk places her thumb and index finger in her mouth. A loud whistle splits the air. Footsteps approach from the distance. Bill watches bleached overalls appear out of nowhere. They all nod toward their table, to Hawk. One by one, they form a line at the pink van, chattering and ordering food from the dancing cook.

When Hawk leans over the table and moves the corn chips closer to Bill, he finally reaches for one and shoves it in his mouth. All these people. All this time. Living in peace and harmony. No guns. No knives. How are they still alive?

Hawk reaches for his hand, squeezes it briefly. "You can't cure the hateful with more hate. Where there's war, chaos, and corruption, sometimes the peaceful and kind must take cover. But never *think* that we wouldn't be here. And never assume we wouldn't be stronger than them."

A scent of brown sauce and potatoes greets them as they enter the mansion's front hallway. Bill kicks off his shoes while Maria heads straight into the kitchen and looks at the dinner plates on trays, set on the kitchen island.

"Micky, if you feed them in their rooms, they'll never see daylight. You know this, right?"

Stirring a soup pot, Micky shrugs his shoulders, not bothering to turn around.

"Or maybe they're just hiding from your overly cheerful and optimistic personality."

The orange Maria throws misses Micky's face, but only by an inch. It hits the cupboard and then lands on the floor, where it rolls under a cupboard. Bill turns away to hide his smile.

Maria grabs a paring knife and sits down on a barstool. As she sinks the knife into the orange skin, she says, "Who's on night shift tonight?"

Just as quickly as it had arrived, the fleeting moment of relaxation is gone.

The trailer.

"I think Earl is. Bill, you traded shifts with him, didn't you?" Micky asks him. He's too focused on the boiling pot to notice how panic rises and takes over Bill's face and body. Maria chews on a piece of orange, her eyes fixed on Bill. As usual, she's noticed the mood change instantly. She can probably hear the panic shaking Bill's core.

The kids.

Bill speed-walks to his loafers, lying in the middle of the front hallway as they usually are. "Earl won't head out for a few hours, right?"

Maria cocks her head, her sharp eyes drilling into Bill's worried face.

"Right?" Bill asks again, his voice slightly too loud. Maria might have been unusually kind to him lately. Still, he's painfully aware that the woman would have no problem snapping his neck or poisoning his morning coffee, if only for yelling at her.

A steady pressure starts at the back of his head. Is Kaarina tapping him? Has she forgiven him? Bill opens the connection, and Maria's soft words echo through his skull.

"Whatcha hiding, Billy-boy? Something you want to share with the rest of the class?"

Not once has she ever tapped Bill before. Not once in two years.

Oblivious to their telepathic conversation, Micky lifts the pot off the stove and places it on the kitchen island. He sinks a white-handled ladle into the rich stew. "Earl likes to start his shifts early. The blood-driven dog he is. I think he takes off as soon as the sun goes down. Maybe if he got out of that creepy shed of his once and awhile, he wouldn't be so . . . Bill?"

But only the loafers remain where Bill had been standing. He has already run out of the door and through the man-made hole in the fencing.

His bare feet sink into the dead grass and rotting fruit. The sweet scent of moldering oranges pierces his nose. Heart beating wildly against his chest, he hurries toward the trailer. Will he find Earl? Before the guard finds what hides underneath the east side's avocado trees?

Bill runs as fast as he can. The oranges give way to avocados. The yellow trailer is just a small dot of light in the distance. Why would the family keep the light on? Do they even know they're trespassing?

Bill gets closer, his footsteps soft against the dry grass. Then he sees Earl there, right outside the outline of the tucked-away trailer. Crickets singing are the only sound around. The coyotes have fled to hunt elsewhere in the tense, heavy air of the early night.

Bill cautiously approaches the trees encircling the trailer. Careful not to get too close, Bill kneels behind the same avocado tree where he hid from the trailer woman and her shotgun only a day before.

Slowly, he pokes his head out. Earl has his slightly hunched back pressed against the wall of the trailer. In his weathered hands, Earl holds an old rifle that usually rests against storage boxes in his small guard shed.

Inside, the sound of kids laughing seems to come from underwater. No reaction from Earl. No shock or hesitation appears in his steady movements. He knows there are children there. He knows he's about to slaughter a whole family.

He doesn't care.

Bill reaches for his Glock. He turns slowly, presses his side against the avocado tree's trunk, and aims the gun at Earl's head. But who is he kidding? He would never hit a target so small. Not from this far away. Bill lowers the gun a few inches, aims at the old man's torso.

Maybe with beginner's luck . . .

A mouthwatering aroma reaches Bill's nose. Spices, fried things . . . it reminds him of the divine meal Sly-Taco prepared him at the winery. Would Hawk take the family in? Would it be too risky to have children so young running around? "No newbies," the old woman had said. But surely she'd make an exception?

Earl turns around slowly. With heavy steps, he backs up to get a better view. He lifts his gun. Bill squeezes the Glock harder. Hands shaking uncontrollably, Bill aims at Earl's silhouette.

But he's too far off. He needs to get closer.

Suddenly, Earl stumbles onto something on the ground. Bill makes his move. He crawls through the rotting avocados and hides behind another tree.

Muffled cursing reaches his ears. A loud yell and Earl falls on his ass. Like he's possessed by a demon, he crab walks away from something on the ground, his chest and belly pointing toward the night sky.

A bright light attached to the trailer's side comes on.

A low rattling sound fills the air.

The trailer door flies open.

A gun fires.

The trailer woman shoots the rattlesnake before it has another go at Earl's leg.

Once the rattling stops, she moves the barrel of her gun to point it at Earl. Keeping her eyes on the stranger, the woman walks sideways to the dead rattlesnake. After kicking it twice, she looks at Earl and says, "Who are you? What do you want from us?"

Earl sits up and raises his hands in the air. "I mean no harm, ma'am. I was only passing through, getting a couple of avocados for the missus." He's trying to sound careless and reassuring, but Bill can tell the rattlesnake has knocked him off his game.

Earl gets up on his knees. He tries a smile, but it comes out as a painful grin. "I wish my wife's cooking smelled like that. Most days, I go to bed with my belly full of brown sauce and potatoes."

The woman lowers the gun but only an inch. Behind the trailer door, three curious heads peek out to see what's going on. Over her shoulder, the woman hisses something in Spanish. The curious eyes disappear back inside the trailer.

She quickly turns her eyes back to Earl. "If you're just picking up fruit, why are you carrying a rifle?"

Earl sits down on the ground. While holding his bitten ankle between his hands, Earl searches the ground for his missing gun. When he spots it, he chuckles and points at the dead snake.

"Why do you think? Those suckers are everywhere these days. This one really caught me by surprise. It's like they're getting smarter and smarter." Panic echoes from Earl's voice.

Earl gets on his knees. The woman's gun raises to aim at his head.

Earl shows the inside of his palms. "Whoa, hey. No need to point that thing at me. If I don't get this leg treated, I'm as good as dead anyway. Besides, you don't want to shoot an innocent man in front of those kids of yours, do you?"

While the woman keeps her weapon trained on the old man on his knees, her partner peeks out of the trailer again. As he whispers in Spanish, the woman responds sharply back to him.

Favoring his injured leg, Earl stands up. His hands lifted, he gestures toward the dead snake on the ground.

The woman lowers her gun another inch. "My partner is asking how bad your injury is."

Earl bends over to investigate his ankle.

The old man lifts his pant leg. Bill could swear he sees Earl's face turn paper white. "The sucker got me real good," Earl says. "I hope I don't end up losing this leg. Anything in that trailer to make a splint? I need to keep my leg as still as possible."

The woman lowers her shotgun to knee level. Stretching her neck, she tries to see Earl's injury in the dark. The brown-haired man peeks out of the trailer, and two little heads follow. He speaks in fast words and waves his hand, gesturing for Earl and the woman to come in.

The woman's gun lowers to point at the ground. "Yeah, we got something. For snake bites. Come on in, but don't expect us to feed you. There's barely enough food for the four of us."

"I thank you kindly," Earl mutters. Bill holds his breath. It's unlikely that Earl wouldn't shoot the family. Not even after they helped him save his leg and possibly his life. No, he'd finish the job and then focus on the snakebite. Knowing Earl, his ego would tell him the bite isn't as deadly to him as it is to most snakebite victims.

Bill holds onto his gun.

The woman hangs the shotgun over her shoulder and turns around. As she starts toward the trailer's door, where the rest of her family digs for materials to make a splint for the stranger in pain, Earl takes a few awkward strides toward his weapon.

Bill gets up and lifts his Glock. He curses under his breath. He aims at Earl, who flicks the rifle's safety. To get a better shot, Bill moves out in the open. He takes a few steps closer. Then a few more. Earl is too focused on his own target to notice Bill's arrival. Or maybe it's the snake bite, starting to make him woozy.

The hunch-backed guard lifts his rifle. The barrel points at the back of the woman's head. As she's about to climb into the trailer, Earl takes a deep inhale, steadies his hands.

The crack of a sniper rifle startles Bill into firing his Glock. The gun kicks back. His poorly aimed bullet breaks one of the trailer's back windows, and he falls on his ass.

By the trailer, Earl's limp body collapses on the ground. His blank face lands next to the dead snake with a *thump*. The trailer door shuts. The lights go off. The woman made it inside. Alive.

Behind Bill's back, a set of smooth footsteps rustle slightly through the dry grass. Women's combat boots stop next to Bill's bare feet. Two strong hands reach under Bill's armpit and, with a single pull, lift Bill to stand on his two feet.

"You shot . . . that was Earl," Bill says.

"I know it was Earl, you dumbass."

"But you . . . I don't . . . why would you . . . "

Absently, like she's not even thinking what her hands are doing, Maria pats some of the rotting avocado off the back of Bill's shirt. Then she takes off her leather gloves and shoves them into Bill's hands.

"You're welcome. Now it's your turn. Clean it up. Toss him off the cliff. Tell them," Maria nods at the trailer, "to find another place to park their trailer."

"My hands won't fit in these tiny-ass gloves."

"So toss them off too. I don't care. Just get it done, Bill."

"And where the hell are you going?" Bill says, his voice raspy and weak.

"I'll be inside, eating Micky's revolting rabbit stew. He's really outdone himself this time."

With those words, she turns to leave. Then, she quickly stops in her tracks. Loud Spanish words hiss between her teeth. "*Hijo de perra . . .*" Maria kicks the ground angrily.

"What is it?"

She gestures toward the orange trees in the distance. Bill sees a shadow running toward the mansion. Maria curses in Spanish and races after whoever has spied on them, surely witnessing Earl's unexpected death.

"Muchas gracias," Alejandro says, for the fourth or fifth time. Together they've rolled Earl's corpse down the cliff. Like a lump of meat, he rolled down the cliff and into the dry stream, along with the dead rattlesnake.

A young girl—Bill thinks she's five or six—jumps down from the trailer and walks straight up to him. Her mother tries to stop her, but Alejandro reaches out and gently pulls the woman back. "*Silvia. Déjala.*"

The girl takes Bill's hand and looks up. A small smile lingers on her round face. "You. Sir. A good man." She then reaches for Bill's leg and gives it a hug. His hands hover around the girl's brown hair, unsure what to do.

Bill swallows the lump in his throat. Managing a nod and a smile, he turns to walk away from the family that cost Earl his life and most likely created a big bundle of problems to solve back at the house.

As he walks away, Hawk's friendly face flashes through his mind. Would the gray woman take these people in? Would Maria ever forgive him if he revealed the secret winery up in the mountains?

His feet stop where Maria took off running toward the mansion. His chin drops, and his shoulders relax. He suddenly feels as if he hasn't slept in weeks. When Bill turns around to face the family of four, the little girl waves at him happily. Bill smiles and waves back.

He clears his throat and lets out a deep sigh.

"You guys like tacos?"

Thoughts muddled in his head, Bill races back to the mansion, following Maria's footsteps. Not knowing what's about to happen now is worse than knowing he has fucked up with Earl and the trailer people. Big time.

Did the person spying on them see who shot Earl? Even if they didn't, how could they explain to the others how an ex-military, well-seasoned killer ended up dead during a routine night shift patrol? What would Bill tell Texas?

As Bill slips through the hole in the wire fencing, he hears shouting inside the mansion. The front door is cracked open; a woman yells loudly while Micky's voice repeatedly responds in a calmer tone.

The front door closes behind Bill with a *bang*. Melissa, the logistics manager, Maria, and Micky turn to look at him. The air is so tense it could be cut with a knife—like the paring knife Melissa's pointing at Maria's throat. "You. You were there. You're the CEO, you have to tell us the truth. Did Maria kill Earl? Or was it the intruder?"

So Melissa's the spy. Great.

"What makes you think it was Maria?" Bill asks.

"I just asked you, Maria or the intruder. Which one?"

"What makes you think that it wasn't me?"

Melissa rolls her eyes.

The sound of muffled footsteps upstairs reaches Bill's ears. He glances up. The rest of the tenants have come out of their solitude to see what the shouting is about. Jada leans over the railing and looks. Once she sees Melissa, she says, "Earl's *dead*? What the hell happened?"

Melissa brings the knife even closer to Maria. "Her. That's what happened. She shot Earl like he was a rat in the barnyard."

Maria rubs the bridge of her nose. She turns and walks into the kitchen, sits on a barstool.

Melissa follows her, waving the knife at her. "Don't you dare walk away. If you have some bullshit explanation for your actions, now is the time. We'll call Jenkins no matter what. And you—" Melissa turns and points the knife at Bill. "You're supposed to be our leader. It's only fair you report this to Jenkins. I don't care what kind of a sick deal you two have going on."

"Hear that, Billy-boy? We have a sick deal. How about that." Maria smiles while she taps Bill. Bill's too tongue-tied to answer, his mind twisted into a messy knot. Shrugging her shoulder, Maria grabs an orange and starts peeling it with her bare hands. Juice splatters around the kitchen table and on her black T-shirt.

Jada walks down the spiral stairs. The rest of the tenants follow her. Only Arturo is missing. They all stop to stand by Melissa. Together, they form a front between Bill, Micky, and Maria. Nobody says a word—like they've forgotten how to speak during their two years spent mostly in solitude.

Bill stares at Maria, waiting for her to speak up. It feels weird to tap her, even more bizarre when she accepts the connection and lets Bill inside her head. *Maria, come on. Tell them the trailer woman shot him. What else can we do? Maria? Oh, you stubborn fuck! Put the orange down and join in the chaos, would you?*

But Maria keeps peeling the orange, a bored expression lingering on her face. *"And then what? They'll hunt them down and kill the whole family? You saw their trailer. It'll take them forever to get out of town."*

Micky joins Maria. "Let's all calm down and take a breather. Earl was a scumbag, but he was still one of us. None of us would ever harm one of our own. So, it must have been the scavenger who killed Earl. Right, Maria?"

She doesn't squirm under their burning gazes. Just shrugs once and pops a piece of orange into her mouth.

Abby goes right up to Maria. "Just tell us. There's still time to go after this asshole. Unless it really was you."

"Or Bill," Bill says. "Maybe it was Bill."

They all ignore him.

Maria rolls her eyes at Abby. "What do you want me to say? Accidents happen? Let's all be real here. None of you are sad that the old grunt's no longer with us."

Radley huffs and walks to the kitchen. He pulls out a bread knife and turns to face Maria. "I don't care if anyone's sad. And I don't care about Earl. But I also don't care to live in the same house with a murderer."

Bill can't help himself. A chuckle escapes his lips. They all turn to stare at him. He spreads his hands and says, "I'm sorry, but *really*? Aren't we *all* murderers?"

"And some murderers we got here," Maria says. "Most of you are all thumbs."

"We all need to calm—"

"Tell me to calm down one more time, Micky, I swear to god."

The seriousness of Melissa's voice makes Bill swallow. This is not good. Melissa still has a knife in her hand. This will end badly. Not for Maria, but anyone who would be foolish enough to attack her.

With a few long strides, Melissa's in front of Maria. Suddenly, the dark woman stands up and leans against the redhead's knife. "Okay, yes. I shot the old fart. Got rid of his body to hide my tracks. What exactly are you going to do about it?"

Tears of anger shine in Melissa's eyes. "I can't believe this. That you'd ruin this place like this. You know this will be the end for all of us. I don't want to be sent into the city to live in some institute. None of us do. I like it here. This is home. And now you two have fucked it all up for all of us." She doesn't lower the knife. Her hand shakes uncontrollably. The air in the room is still and stale. Bill holds his breath, knowing that everyone around him is doing the same.

Maria, take a step back. Please.

Maria repositions herself and leans forward even further. The knife now digs into the skin above her collarbone. A drop of blood travels down and into her black T-shirt.

What are you doing? Just step away. You're bleeding, for fuck's sake.

A tear travels down Melissa's freckled face.

A few long strides and Bill's in the kitchen. He blinks rapidly, clearing his throat. "Maria didn't shoot Earl. I did. Okay? I shot Earl because he was about to slaughter two kids and their parents, whose only sin was to enter through the wrong fucking fence. Maria just happened to be there. But it was me who pulled the trigger, not her."

Melissa pulls her knife and turns to Bill.

"You are one sick fuck, you know that? Who kills one of their own? Earl did nothing wrong. We're supposed to shoot intruders and protect the farm. If we don't, we'd all be stuck in the Chip-Center. You know this, Bill. We all do. Jenkins is giving us a good deal. A home. What kind of a person doesn't protect their own home?"

"From what? From two little kids and their—"

A voice from the staircase interrupts Bill's reply. Arturo walks down the stairs and stops halfway down. "You should never have been the CEO, William. We've all been here longer than you." Black-green AR-glasses hang from his left hand. "I've been here the longest. It's me who should be moving to the city first. Not you." He lifts up the blinking glasses and winces.

"But better late than never. I called Jenkins and told him his golden boy executed one of the mansion's own . . . And I just got bumped up the list."

CHAPTER 5
DOWN THE STREAM

Everyone but Micky, Maria, and Bill follow Arturo upstairs and lock themselves in their bedrooms to wait for justice to be done. Texas has sent someone to pick Bill up from the mansion.

"This is bullshit," Micky mumbles, his spoon making figure eights in the lukewarm stew in front of him. He seems calm, but Bill knows better. Micky's always afraid when Bill visits the city. And this time he might not be coming back.

After the blowout, Micky had set down three bowls, three spoons, and an oversized pot of stew. None of them have been able to eat any.

"Total bullshit," Micky says again. "What if they won't let you come back?"

"I'll come back. I got something to barter with. Don't worry so much. I got this."

Maria looks up from her bowl. "No, I'm with Micky. You're not exactly the best negotiator, to say the least." Her elbows rest against the table, her palms supporting her tired face. It's the first time Bill has ever witnessed Maria being anything but energetic and full of it. Piss and vinegar. Mad and troubled. Never like this: worn-out and jaded.

Micky's spoon clinks against the porcelain bowl. "It's bullshit that Texas wouldn't come here to hear us out himself. Why do you have to go to the city? Is there going to be a trial or something? Who is this *someone* he's sending over? What if they're not interested in bartering with you, beau?"

Bill puts his spoon down. He slides the cold stew forward on the table. "Can you two relax, please? I know how to deal with Texas. They won't shove me into a capsule. Not when I'm connected with Kaarina."

"And what happens when they find her?" Maria asks. Micky nods repeatedly, his eyes flickering between Bill and Maria.

"I'll be back home by then," Bill says, but his voice is lacking the confidence he wishes he had. He has no plan. Not even the slightest. There's no way he'd sell out Kaarina, even if he knew where she was. But there's also no way that he'll let Texas hold Maria responsible for Earl's death.

"You shouldn't have done that. Taken the blame," Maria says. She looks at Micky, shaking her head slightly. "It wasn't Bill who shot Earl. It was me."

Micky guffaws. "You think I don't know that?" He chuckles and points his spoon at Bill. "Loverboy here wouldn't have managed to shoot Earl's fat head even if his gun was pressed against the poor bastard's temple."

Maria joins Micky's laughter. Bill rolls his eyes but can't help but smile.

"When do you think they'll come?" Micky spoons up a bit of the cold stew, his hand shaking slightly.

"Micky, relax." Bill curses his voice, still too weak and doubtful. "It'll all be okay."

"They'll have all kinds of devices and lie detectors and—"

"Micky, stop," Maria says. She lets her spoon drop against the plate. "And fuck Texas. He should have hauled his fat ass up here himself. If this dingleberry here hadn't taken the blame, I could have lied my way out of it. Easily. I could, but not you. We all know you're a terrible liar."

Bill looks up and blinks rapidly. "I am not."

The stew bursts out of Micky's mouth. "Oh, really? Okay then. Tell me, how many night shifts have you spent hiding inside the barn?"

Bill squints his eyes at him. "None."

"Okay. Why is that?"

Bill squirms in his seat, dodging Maria's amused gaze. She's now spooning the stew with an appetite. No sign of her momentary hopelessness remains.

"I don't know. Maybe there was never anyone trespassing."

"Ha! So easy. Your first answer was true. The second is bullshit."

"Oh, what do you know."

"I know because you have a tell."

Maria chuckles and shakes her head at their quarreling. She lifts the bowl and licks the edges.

Bill reaches for his bowl and starts spooning the brown liquid up, just to give his hands something to do. Stew dripping from the corner of his mouth, he says, "I do not have a tell."

"Yeah, you do," Maria says. "Even white lies that don't mean a thing get you blinking like a maniac."

Bill focuses on his eyelids, forces them to stay still. "Bullshit, you ass-hat." He blinks twice.

Micky and Maria's laughter fills the kitchen.

Maria leans over to Micky. "I'll tell you why Billy-boy here never offed anyone. Except for the girl that scored him the promotion. It's not because he would have hidden in the barn during his shifts. It's because I covered his ass—did each of his patrols for him. Some people are better off staying inside after dark. And I shouldn't have to point this out after today's events."

Micky huffs and drops his spoon. "You never do any of my shifts! No matter what I have going on."

"Yeah, but Earl did. I know neither of you got out there much. All you pussies can handle is drawing stupid-ass pictures for stupid-ass city people," Maria nods at Bill, "and burning food on the stove," she nods at Micky. Micky throws his spoon at Maria. She catches it midair.

"Bill?"

At the sound of Kaarina's voice inside his head, Bill jumps off his seat and leaves the room. Maria and Micky keep chattering. Bill never noticed Kaarina tapping him. How long has she been listening? What made her come back?

"I'm here. Kaarina. I'm here. Listen, I never meant—"

"You can't let them take you to the city, Bill. You know what will happen."

Bill clears his throat and walks in circles around his loafers, still lying in the middle of the front hallway. "We don't know what's going to happen, but I have to go and see, or else they'll take Maria instead."

"I know. I heard. I know what happened."

In his mind, Bill goes through the conversations he's had with his mansion friends over the last hour. What had he said? What had Kaarina overheard? That he'd take the blame. That Texas would surely let him walk if he only—

"Kaarina, I didn't mean it. I won't tell them where you are. I don't even *know* where you are. And don't tell me, I don't—"

"I'm down at the old harbor. In a city that used to be called Turku. I'll wait for Doctor Solomon's men here. Yeti wants to fight them. I don't, but I'm willing to do what it takes. Just don't let them take you to the Chip-Center. You don't belong in that capsule, Bill. You need to get out. Leave the mansion. Help others see what the city is doing to us. You are a good person, no matter what they've made you do in the past. I know about the brown-haired girl. I was there, you just didn't notice. And it's okay. I get it. I get you. And that's why you need to trust me when I say that you have to stay out of that capsule, no matter what it takes. People need you, Bill. Someone needs to be crazy enough to believe they can beat Solomon's ass."

Bill opens his mouth to argue but freezes to listen. The mansion's front gates creak open. A set of van tires rolls up the mansion's driveway.

Four guards wearing green overalls walk in. They all carry a gun on one side of their green belts and a tranquilizer gun on the other. Bill had been expecting one person—a cab driver of sorts—not four armed guards to escort him to the city. He had assumed that Texas would play this civil. Clearly, he's mistaken. They will get the truth out of him, one way or another. And they won't stop until Kaarina is captured.

No matter how many tells he has or what equipment the van holds for his torture, Bill can keep the information to himself—for now. But once he's back in the city, their brain scanners will surely dig the truth out in a matter of minutes.

Micky and Maria walk into the front hallway. They stare at the guards but walk straight to Bill. Micky leans over and half-whispers into his ear, "What the shit is this?"

Maria crosses her arms on her chest. Frowning, she leans in closer to Bill and hisses, "This isn't what we agreed upon, Bill. Let me tell them it was me."

"Not a chance. I got this. So they sent more than one guy. This doesn't change anything. Now back off, both of you."

Maria searches his eyes. Almost pleading, she says, "Just let me go instead. You stay. Be a graphic designer for a change."

Bill has a sudden urge to hug her. But allies or not, she'd still probably knock him out cold if he was to enter her personal space.

"I'll be back before you know it," he says. Then he walks to the guards, raising his hands in a gesture of surrender. "Okay, boys. Let's get going. I heard the city has new vegan cheesecake, and I'm dying to give it a go." He walks to the closest guard, offers him his wrists. "Shall we?"

The guard nods, not at Bill but someone he's talking to through his AR-glasses. He takes the glasses off and looks at Bill with a dull expression on his face. "Just wait in that corner with your friends, pal. We'll get to you soon. Where are the others?"

"What? No. Who?"

"The rest of Mister Jenkins's employees. Are they upstairs?"

"Why? What's going on?" Bill asks. "We would like to talk to Dennis himself."

"That's a negative. Mister Jenkins is not available at the moment."

"But he's in charge here," Maria says.

The guard scoffs and turns his back on them. "Not when Laura Solomon's in town."

Dumbfounded, they stare at the waxy, pale-skinned guard, nodding toward the staircase. "They're upstairs. Get the van going and lock it with a fresh CS-key."

Bill backs away from the guard until he's standing with Maria and Micky again. Astounded, all three watch as the guards run upstairs and start kicking in the bedroom doors.

"Should we go help them?" Micky whispers.

"You'll have a dart on your back the second you move toward the door," Maria says. "Just stay put."

Screams and yells echo around the usually quiet mansion. One by one, Abby, Jack, Melissa, Arturo, Jada, and Radley are brought downstairs. Their hands are tied behind their backs with CS-finger-cuffs.

The van door slams shut. Three of the guards return inside. The fourth guard yells from the mansion's front yard, "Hey! Where's the CS-key?"

The three guards ignore their colleague's question and move in for Bill, Maria, and Micky, still standing by the front hallway's pantry closet.

"Seriously, I can't find it. Are you sure we brought one?"

Without warning, Maria charges the closest guard, grabbing for his gun. They land hard on the floor, Maria pinning down the wax-faced man. The two other guards turn to look at the struggle on the floor, but only for a brief second. Then they charge at Bill and Micky. The white ceiling spins while Bill wrestles with the guard. He kicks and hits, his hands and legs thrashing wildly in the air. He's not a fighter, but he's damned if he'll go without a fight.

A gun goes off. Then another. Bill's fight with the guard continues. He reaches for the guard's face and shoves his finger deep into the man's eye. Yelling curse words, the guard rolls off Bill and onto the floor. One hand covering his eye, his free hand reaches for the tranquilizer gun. Maria appears out of nowhere. She snatches the tranquilizer from the guard's hand and shoots the dart into his neck. Then a third shot echoes against the hallway's walls.

Maria's body falls limp on top of the drugged guard.

Bill turns around to see a bleeding guard, his gun now pointing at him. He aims at Bill but passes out in the puddle of his own blood before his finger can pull the trigger again. The gun falls from his hand. Micky crawls toward the gun, a stream of blood gushing from his shoulder. He collapses on the floor, motionless.

All three guards lie lifeless on the mansion's floor. Maria and Micky too. When the fourth guard rushes in, Bill presses his face against the floor and pretends to be dead.

Bill's hand shakes uncontrollably as he brings the paring knife up to Micky's shoulder. He looks at the partly empty tranquilizer dart next to Micky's bloody shirt. Did he give him enough? Will the sedative help Micky pull through what's about to happen?

After the fourth guard walked calmly out of the mansion and back to his van, Bill helped Micky upstairs and into Bill's walk-in closet. Now Micky lies here, barely conscious under the neat row of suits and jackets hanging against the dimly lit wall.

Has Bill ever worn any of this stuff? The designer outfits and accessories? He wouldn't have. Not since he moved into the mansion. Right at this moment, his belongings—the gold wristwatches, diamond rings, and fancy footwear—make him sick to his stomach. Or maybe it's the sickening task he's about to take on.

The knife digs into the bullet wound in Micky's shoulder. Bill has no idea what he's doing. Just what he's seen in the movies and TV shows when those things still had their time and place in life. But he knows that if he doesn't remove the bullet, Micky's odds are about as good as those of a rat crossing paths with Earl.

A gush of blood bursts out. Bill inserts the tweezers and searches around for the bullet. When his stomach flips more violently, Bill turns around and vomits on a pair of Testoni dress shoes. Out of breath and terrified of passing out, he reaches for a tuxedo tail and wipes his mouth. He forces himself to focus on the mumbling and grunting Micky. Half asleep, half awake, Micky murmurs something in Spanish.

Bill moves the tweezers in the wound until they clink on something hard. Probing and fishing, he's unable to get the bullet between the tweezers to pull it out.

"Oh, for fuck's sake . . ."

As he sinks his thumb and index finger into Micky's flesh, his drugged companion's eyes fly open. As Micky starts to yell in pain, Bill reaches for a two-thousand-dollar Valentino dress shirt and pulls it off its hanger. He shoves the sleeve into Micky's mouth.

"I'm so sorry, buddy. Fuck, fuck, fuck. I'm so. Freaking. Sorry."

He keeps digging. Bill grasps the bullet and moves it up and out of Micky's shoulder. He tosses it on the table in the middle of the room. The bullet lands in the middle of a neat row of watches and rings. From there, it falls on the floor with a *clink*.

Bill pulls down another dress shirt and rips it into shreds. After knotting the pieces together, he carefully adjusts the tourniquet to stop the bleeding. At some point while he's been working, Micky has passed out.

He sets a pile of shoeboxes in front of Micky and the puddle of Micky's blood. Bullet-free and barely conscious, the injured man now lies under Bill's useless fashion collection. Bill leaves the walk-in closet and shuts the sliding door behind him. He leans against the door and listens for sounds from downstairs.

Quiet. Just like the mansion normally is.

He tiptoes to the open balcony doors. Outside, he lowers his body and crawls to the railing. He slowly pokes his head out. A guard talks into an AR-set by a van parked next to the mansion's front door. The van's door is shut, but no CS-key locks it. The rest of Bill's roommates are inside, unable to open the door. But Bill could open it. If he can get to the van before the guard drives away.

Bill returns inside. He stares at his Glock for a moment. Shaking his head, he then takes the gun and runs back to the walk-in closet. Once he has placed the gun in the now unconscious Micky's hand, he runs out of the room and to the stairs.

Downstairs, four bodies lay in a puddle of blood. The metallic smell makes Bill gag. Careful not to look at Maria's cold, lifeless body, he runs to the closest dead guard and grabs the tranquilizer dart from his gun.

A green fabric bag lies on the floor next to Bill's loafers. Bill reaches for it and pulls out bottles of medicine, puts them in his pocket. When his hand finds his CS-key, he shoves it into the back of his pants. Then he rushes to the front door.

Outside, the guard has ended his AR-call. He's leaning against the van, smoking a cigarette. Bill's bare feet tread silently in the soil by the rose bushes. He thinks of Maria, how she moves in such a ghostly way. *Moved*. With grace and lightness. Why had it freaked him out so badly?

Why had he judged Maria to be some cold-blooded excuse for a human being? All she ever did was fight for her existence. Maria wasn't black and white—cruel—like Bill had considered her to be. For the past two years, her life has been about balancing what needs to be done to survive with what she could pull off to help others.

Before his eyes begin to water, Bill circles the van, the tranquilizer wrapped in his fist. He doesn't give himself time to overthink. He charges for the smoking guard. The guard turns quickly. He throws his fist at Bill's jaw, sending him flying. He falls on his back. His head hits the gravel hard, and the tranquilizer Bill brought from inside flies into the rose bushes.

The guard reaches for his gun but can't find it. His quick glance at the van tells Bill he must have abandoned his weapons while looking for the missing CS-key. The guard thought he was the only one alive—he and the hostages in the back of the van.

The guard takes a step closer. "Jenkins said to bring you in alive. But I've had enough Unchipped crap for one day." He grabs Bill by the front of his shirt. While the guard pulls his fist back, Bill reaches around to the back of his pants.

The metal CS-key blocks the guard's fist. The impact makes the guard jump back and scream in pain. He falls on his ass.

Bill jumps up and runs to the van. He opens the passenger side door and rummages through the seats in the dark. Then he finds what he's looking for: the green weapon belt has fallen between the seats. As he reaches for the tranquilizer gun, the guard grabs him by the collar, pulls him back. The belt slips from Bill's fingers. It falls deeper into the gap between the seats.

"Can't you just die already?" the guard hisses between his teeth. He turns Bill around and lands his fist on Bill's left eye. Then on his jaw. On the right eye. Back on his jaw. Bill's arms fall limp by his sides. The guard pushes him against the passenger seat. Spit lands on Bill's forehead and half-closed eyelids.

"Unchipped scum."

The lights blink on the guard's AR-glasses, hanging by his neck. He jerks back to put them on. "Yeah? Good. About time. It's getting ridiculous out here."

Bill relaxes his body, lets it sink into the van's leather seat. When his hand drops limp by his side, it lands on something hard and cold. The guard's gun. It has slipped from its holster and onto the van's floor.

Bill grabs the gun and prays it works the same way as his Glock, tucked upstairs in his walk-in closet next to unconscious Micky. He points the gun at the guard, aims as well as his blurred vision allows, and pulls the trigger. Blood splatters from the guard's skull. He falls back, dead on the mansion's driveway.

Bill gets out of the van. Angrily, he steps on the AR-glasses by the dead guard's body, trying to crush them with his bare feet. The only thing that's getting crushed is the callus on his heel, so he kicks the AR-glasses as hard as he can. They land in the bushes under Melissa's bird feeders.

"Melissa . . . "

A few strides and Bill's by the van's rear doors. He knocks on the door repeatedly. "It's me. Bill. If one of you has a gun in there, don't shoot me. Okay? I'm coming in."

He opens the van doors. Radley, Jada, and Abby sit closest to the doors. Their dilated, drugged eyes look at Bill without seeing a thing. Jack and Melissa lie at the back of the van, tucked into a wide gurney. Arturo stands in the middle, staring at Bill with wide eyes.

Bill gestures to him to come out. "You okay? Is anyone hurt?"

With slow, careful steps, Arturo walks out of the van and jumps to the driveway. His hands pull at his overgrown hair. His eyes look bewildered. "They're crazy, Bill. Dead-on sadistic. They were making *jokes* about it. How all of us would soon be a bunch of zombies. Stuffed inside stasis capsules and forgotten in a basement. What the hell is this, Bill? What's going on?"

Bill's hand hovers above Arturo's shoulder. He's unsure whether it'd be okay to touch the man or not. Considering Arturo's been locked inside his bedroom for most of the last two years, Bill lowers his hand. "The city's not what it seems. It's all connected. City of California. The uprising at the headquarters. They all work together. Shutting Unchipped into stasis capsules to get rid of us."

Arturo lifts his gaze and stares at Bill. "And we can't go to Texas, can we?"

"Who do you think arranged this little persecution? No, we can't go to Jenkins. He's involved, big time. He's the one who sent this van and told these guards to come here."

"What then? Where are we supposed to go?"

Bill's eyes scan the gravel. Once he finds what he's looking for, he sprints to get the CS-key and hands it to Arturo. "Do you know how to use one of these?"

When Arturo nods, Bill continues. "Insert your handprint and lock the van door. It'll work without a chip, Jenkins' special settings. Then drive down the valley, continue to the east side of the mountains, and head up until you see an old winery. It'll look abandoned, but it isn't. Look for a pink taco stand. Ask for Hawk or Marco. Tell them . . . that

Maria sent you. That it was her last wish for them to take you in."

Arturo snaps out of his trance and starts entering commands into the CS-key's computer. Then he hurries back to the van's door, slams the CS-key on its designated spot, and waits.

A green light starts blinking on the metal plate.

"Now go. They've sent more guards. You don't have much time."

Arturo hurries to the driver's seat. Just before he slams the door shut, he pokes his head out. A deep frown makes his face look years older than it did only a few hours before.

"What about you? You're not coming with us?"

Bill's eyes flicker to the railing of his bedroom balcony.

"Not today. I left something valuable upstairs that I won't leave behind."

On his back, Bill lies in the middle of the walk-in closet and waits.

Waits for the guards and their heat detection cameras. Waits for Texas and a stasis capsule with Bill's name on it. The Glock's weight presses the back of his hand into the cool floor. At least he has an option.

Micky snores lightly, still tucked under the suits and tuxedos, covered by a pile of shoe boxes. Bill might have saved his life by dragging him upstairs and digging out the bullet from his shoulder. But wouldn't Micky have been better off dying downstairs next to Maria? At least it would have quickened his end.

Bill stares at the top shelves, where piles of cardboard boxes collect dust and cobwebs. His drawings. Portraits and landscapes of people and places he used to see and visit. Everyone he's ever cared for is gone. Dead, or at least dying. Just like Maria. Just like Micky.

Ignoring Kaarina's fierce tapping, Bill closes his eyes and lets the murky waters swallow him up. But this is not one of his episodes. Not part of him being bipolar, needing medication to cope with his own rollercoaster of a mind.

This is him being a fuckup.

If he hadn't hidden behind an avocado tree and let a rabbit save his pathetic life, Earl would still be alive. And so would Maria. He wouldn't have jeopardized Hawk and her people by sending not just one but two vehicles to their secret location.

He presses his thumbs into his sore, swollen eyes and fights the tears. A sob escapes his cracked lips. He would take another beating in a heartbeat. If it brought Maria back. He would take three beatings. Five. A hundred.

All this time in the mansion, he has focused on the bad things, everything that has gone wrong. The lack of privacy. His unrewarding job. The night shifts. Bill has been so fixated on hating this place that he never saw the good in it: the hummingbirds. Micky's small but caring gestures. Maria's half-smiles and her unique friendship. Bill should have stopped to read between the lines.

Friends. Food and shelter. Laughter. Home.

Micky murmurs something in his sleep. His head turns to the side, and for a second, his eyes open to look at Bill. When he smiles, Bill smiles back, not sure what to say. At least Micky's so out of if there's no need to tell him what's to come. Bill closes his fingers around the Glock.

The knock on the bedroom door startles him. When has another van arrived? He has been so deep in thought, he's missed the sounds. Shouts out front. Body bags being dragged across the hallway and onto the driveway. Someone with a body heat scanner, walking up the stairs.

The door muffles a woman's calm voice. She speaks with a thick accent Bill recognizes with ease. It's the same as Kaarina's.

"William? You in there? Open the door, dear."

The sound of blood rushing in his ears makes it hard to block Kaarina's tapping. Bill's distracted. Tired. Drained.

Another knock. "Bill? This is Doctor Solomon. I'm here to help you. You're making things way worse for yourself than needed, my love."

Micky's eyes open again, staring softly at Bill. Lifting his index finger to his lips, Bill gestures to Micky to stay quiet. Then he gets up, places the Glock back in Micky's hand, and exits the walk-in closet. Slow, hesitant steps take him to the bureau that blocks anyone from entering his bedroom. Carefully, he leans his bruised forehead over the narrow but heavy bureau and on the door.

"Listen, Bill. All I need is a bit of help. To bring my people back home. They left City of Finland, thinking something bad was going to happen to them. That the city would somehow hurt their wellbeing. But all the Happiness-Program ever brought them was a second chance to have a normal life."

Bill closes his eyes.

"They got scammed, dear. Brainwashed by someone mentally ill. Someone delusional. Kaarina needs help, Bill. She needs both of us. She's erratic. If we don't find her, she's going to end up hurting a lot of people. Herself included. Help us help her. Let's bring our girl back home.

Then we can all get back to healing and living our lives to the fullest."

Her pleasant, soft voice reminds Bill of his own mother. A voice so reassuring and friendly, it tempts him to open the door. To let her take him back to the city.

"If you tell me where our mutual friend is located, I'll talk to Mister Jenkins. I'll get you moved into the city. You can get that apartment with a view and everything that is rightfully yours. All the things you were promised on the day of your chipping. I can fix all of this, my dear child. And I can do it tonight."

His hand slides against the bureau. Fingering the doorknob, he hears Micky stepping into the room. He stops behind Bill and places his hand on Bill's shoulder. Knowing it's Micky who taps him now, Bill opens the connection.

"Don't listen to her. You don't need those things. You don't need the city. Not all is lost, Bill. You still have me."

Bill's hand hovers on the doorknob. Images of brown, bloody hair fill his head. Images of gunned down people on the valley's roads. A dead rattlesnake. Dead Earl. Maria.

I fucked up, Micky. They're all dead because of me.

Micky's good arm wraps around Bill. He winces when Micky's hands hold him tighter. He must have broken a rib while taking a beating from the guard. Another person who is dead because of Bill.

"We all do the best we can. Some of us only have the strength and wisdom to protect ourselves. And that's okay. We need to save ourselves first before we can help others. But you, Bill. You tried to help Maria. Refused to reveal Kaarina's location. You saved a family of four from getting slaughtered."

The tears burn his torn face. Drop after drop, they land on the bureau.

"You are stronger than most, Bill. Righteous. Brave. You just needed some time to see what I see. What Maria saw."

Bill pulls his hand from the doorknob and turns to face Micky. Behind the door, Doctor Solomon continues to talk, but her voice is now muffled and distant. Bill doesn't hear a word she says. But he hears Micky. Every single word echoes through his mind.

"Maria saw it. She even said it out loud. That you'd have what it takes to fight against the city. That not all heroes are great shots. That there's a different kind of strength in people who are soft and caring. She believed in you, Bill. She said that if you just got out of your own way, you'd be the first to wake up and see the city for what it really is. And that you'd stand up for those who have lost their way. And I see it too, Bill. You are a good man."

In Bill's mind, a little brown-haired girl jumps out from a yellow trailer. Giggling, she runs around a pink van, lit by red glowing chili peppers. Has the family made it to Hawk alive? Did Arturo?

Bill takes Micky's hand and walks him to the balcony railing. They listen for movement. When they can only hear people downstairs inside the house, Bill climbs over the balcony railing and slides his way to the other end. Micky disappears inside and returns, carrying a black duffel bag.

Fingers wrapped around the lower part of the railing, Bill lets his feet slip off the ledge. He takes a deep breath, gritting his teeth, and lets go of the railing. It seems forever until his feet land in the bushes, spraining his ankle. He gets up and wipes dirt off his injured face.

No motion sensors are activated.

Holding one arm against his chest, Micky flings the duffel bag over the balcony. It lands next to Bill in the bushes. Grinning in pain, Micky follows its lead and lands on his good shoulder. While he curses in Spanish, Bill helps him get up and tosses the duffel bag on his own back.

"It's broken," Micky whispers to him.

"Suck it up, buttercup. We'll get you help but we need to get out of here first. Let's go."

They run. At the barnyard, Bill stops to breathe. He looks over his shoulder. A woman in a white coat leans against his balcony railing, staring in their direction.

The guards' shouts send them running toward the east side of the farm.

The shouts cease as soon as Micky and Bill get to where the orange trees turn into avocados. His world still spinning, Bill carries the bouncing duffel and runs as fast as he can. Micky runs behind him, his pace way slower than Bill's, despite Bill's sprained ankle. He has to keep stopping to wait for Micky to catch up with him.

They get to the hole in the fence. Bill stops and presses his hands against his knees, out of breath and close to collapsing. Micky falls to his knees, holding his arm against his chest.

Bill sets the duffel back on the ground and rummages through the items Micky has thrown in it back in the mansion. He picks out a long-sleeved T-shirt and rips the fabric into long strips. Knotting the ends together, he wraps it around Micky's shoulder and arm.

"We can't stop, Bill," Micky says. "They'll track us down. Easily. Who knows how many men that evil witch brought with her?"

"I know. Micky. Just give me a minute. I'm almost done."

While he ties Micky's shoulder sling, Bill looks around in the moonlight. The dead grass presses against the ground. That's where the trailer was parked, only a few hours back. He turns to look to his right. No tracks of Earl's body in the long grass. Would the corpse still be down by the stream? Or did the guards already collect what the city considered to be rightfully theirs? A piece of hardware in his brain?

"All done." Bill turns to collect the duffel bag from the ground. "And, you're right. We do need to get the hell out of here."

"And go where, exactly? To the valley? Even if your pedicured feet survived the hike, I'd end up bleeding dry."

"You're going to give me shit about my lack of shoes? *Now*?"

"Who knew you'd end up a shoeless hobo?"

"Doesn't really matter what I look like if I'm rotting six feet under, does it?"

A shout in the distance startles them both.

Bill stands up and follows Micky to the hole in the fencing. They push through and take a right, where a narrow path snakes down the mountainside. Bill refuses to check down the stream to see if the Chipped have collected Earl or not. Images of chopped off heads make him run faster.

"Stop thinking stuff like that. You're giving me the creeps."

"Stop tapping me when I'm only two feet away."

They make it down to a paved road. In the dim moonlight, they can't see anyone else around. Are they safe? For now?

Bill throws the duffel bag down and unzips it. "Better get that Glock out. We need to walk through the valley of death."

"Pun intended?"

"More jokes? Really? Just let me find the fucking gun, okay, Micky?"

Micky clears his throat and looks away. "You might not find the gun, Bill."

"What do you mean, I might not find it?" When Micky doesn't reply, Bill continues to rummage through the bag. "It'll still be here. The bag has stayed zipped this whole time."

"You won't find the gun because it's still at the house."

Bill's hands stop moving. "Oh, that's rich. That's cute, Micky." He bounces up and starts pacing in circles. "You're telling me you had time to grab a pile of papers, my freaking drawing tablet, and a change of underwear. But you forget the one thing that just might keep us alive?"

Micky shrugs once, unsure what to say.

"Might as well kill me now!" Bill's hands let go of the duffel bag. It lands on the ground with a *thump*.

At the sound of a racking shotgun, they jump down and take cover. They lie beside the open duffel bag, covering their heads and scanning the darkness around them.

"You see them?"

I don't see shit.

"We're so fucking dead, Micky."

The footsteps come closer. A pair of women's muck boots move toward them and stop a couple feet from Micky's and Bill's trembling bodies.

"You. I know you." The voice sounds vaguely familiar.

Micky stumbles onto his knees. "Please, Miss. We're only passing through. Just let us go. You'll never see us again."

After what seems like a minute of silence, the woman lowers the gun and swings it onto her back. A few strides and the boots stop right in front of Bill's face. She reaches out her hand. His hand shaking, Bill takes it and lets the woman pull him up from the dirt.

"Thanks to you, my children still have a mother. And a father. Alejandro's never fired a gun in his life. Without me, they wouldn't have stood a chance."

Micky looks up. His wild gaze travels from the trailer woman—Silvia—to Bill and then back. "Bill, you know this woman?"

Bill nods but doesn't turn to look at Micky. As he stares at the woman, Bill's smile turns into a grin. "Not a big fan of tacos, then?"

"Not a big fan of being trapped," Silvia says. "No matter how nice the place or who I'm with. We're taking the trailer down south. Tonight. I don't know what else to do."

Bill looks at Micky and gestures him to bring the duffel back over. He digs for his drawing tablet, which is also his personal computer. After he powers it up, he taps in a safety code and enters his CC savings account.

"The south is cluttered with city cameras. I have a better idea."

The yellow trailer zigzags around potholes and debris on the highway. They pass a green sign for San Diego airport. The sign's off its hinges, but still holding on.

His Unchipped friends take turns tapping Bill. It's odd to hear Melissa inside his head, telling him Hawk has agreed to take them in. All the mansion tenants are safely tucked away at the remote winery.

"The Chipped patrols roam all over the village," Melissa says. "The roads are blocked and guarded. They're scanning areas outside the city that they took no interest in before. The drones are far away from us.

But we don't know when they'll change their direction. Bill, this means . . . " Melissa clears her throat, too sad to finish her sentence. "Hawk asked me to tell you . . . "

"I know, Mel. We can't come to you. Not if we want to keep the winery a secret."

In his mind, Bill watches Melissa lower her chin and shake her head. "It's shitty, and I'm sorry. I'm sorry about everything that went down in the mansion, Bill. If there was any other way . . . "

"Don't worry, Mel. We have a plan."

As the yellow trailer bounces over a pothole in the road, Kaarina's thick accent appears in Bill's head. *"We'll pay you back, Bill. Every single CC."*

Bill looks at the open duffel bag on the trailer's floor. A corner of his drawing tablet sticks out between the clothing and papers.

"No, you won't."

"Calling me a liar, Yankee?"

"You won't pay me back because your CCs are no good here."

"How about Yeti's money? Or the rest of the hobos I travel with?"

Did he really once call them that? Kaarina has never said anything about it, but Bill knows she's grown fond of each person she travels with. He shouldn't be calling them names. Especially now that he'll soon be one of them.

"If you call them friends, consider them my friends as well. Yes, even the Yeti."

When he realizes that Kaarina's too stunned to reply, Bill continues. "I'll meet you there. I'm just not sure if this kid you told me about is worth the extra trip. Who is she again?"

"She's one of the Chipped's, Niina's, daughter, stuck in a children's home . . . Bill, it's a long story. I'll tell you once you land."

"Fine, fine. But now that the Chipped are after us, we need to stay undercover. They'll hunt down and capture any Unchipped that live outside the Chip-Centers."

Kaarina nods repeatedly. *"You're right. One of our hackers just reported that City of California has promised a thousand CCs for each Unchipped brought to the city. Dead or alive. But they'll be looking for us in City of Finland and in City of California. Not outside the country. Maybe hiding out in the open is exactly what we should do. It's the last place they'll look."*

"You better be fucking right, Kay. This shit is crazy."

"And you're sure the black market won't leak the information?" Kaarina asks. *"What if the cities track your CC transfers?"*

"The black market is neutral. All purchases are confidential. I've never had an issue with it, and neither did anyone in the mansion. We're good, Kay."

"If you say so. I'm having a hard time trusting anyone these days, but we don't really have an option here, do we?"

Bill shakes his head for no. "And once we land? You never told me the plan."

"I'll tell you face to face. Once we meet. Soon. I'll tell you everything, first thing when you land at Heathrow airport."

Alejandro drives the truck and the yellow trailer on a snaking dirt road. Silvia sits quietly at the front of the trailer. In her arms, she holds a sleeping boy wrapped inside a warm blanket. A brown-haired girl with round eyes sits opposite her brother and mother, staring out the trailer window.

At the back of the trailer, Micky and Bill sit on the lower part of a bunkbed. A pile of clothes, shoes, and toys are all tossed around the trailer like someone let in a pack of partying coyotes.

The mess doesn't bother Bill.

His muddy, blood-stained clothes don't bother him.

His swollen shut eyes, cracked lips, bruised face . . . all the same.

He's alive. With good people. Friends. He's about to meet Kaarina in person. Join her and the rebels she leads into the unknown.

Traffic lights blink yellow. The dark night sky looms wide open in front of them. Another blinking light in the distance grabs their attention. Alejandro takes a right turn and heads toward it.

A jet. Just outside the airport, alone in the middle of a field.

Bill has used all his CCs to fly twenty-six people to City of England. And he didn't even wince when zeroing out his savings account.

He's now poor. Homeless. Strangely hopeful.

Silvia's brown-haired little girl makes her way to Bill. While walking in the bouncing trailer, she supports herself on the kitchen table, the small row of narrow closets, the bunkbed frame. Once she's by Bill's side, she pulls him by the sleeve of his shirt. "Look, sir. *El avión.*" She nods toward the trailer window. "It is, umm . . . it is an airplane."

Bill gives the girl a smile. "That it is. Have you ever been on one?"

The girl shakes her head and sits down in the middle of the clothing pile. With his good hand, Micky pats her head and grins at her. Then he looks at Bill.

"Are you sure this is going to work? I know it's a lot of CCs you paid them. But they also work with the Chipped. What if they sell us out?"

"They won't. This will work, Micky." His eyes fix on the people at a distance, standing by the airplane. "It has to."

Micky stares at the blinking light, getting closer and closer by the minute. His good hand rests still by the side of the bed. The girl's head presses against the back of his palm. She's fighting to keep her eyes open. Despite the excitement and the bouncing trailer, she's falling fast asleep.

"What makes you think that we got what it takes? To live our lives as rebels?"

The trailer makes its way across the field and to the jet plane, where a crowd of five men and women are waiting. They all wear all-black clothes and AR-glasses. The airport in the distance is dimly lit. They're so close, yet light years away from the actual terminal and the people who can travel without taking advantage of black-market services.

They stop by their getaway plane. No one moves a muscle to get out. Bill keeps his eyes on the airplane's blinking light: the one that will soon light their way to City of England.

"I know we have what it takes," Bill says, his eyes calm, unblinking, "because when was Maria ever wrong in her entire life?"

THE END

Shoot! Book 2 of the Unchipped story is at a close. But don't worry, you can find out what happens next in Book 3 in the Unchipped series, UNCHIPPED: ENYD!

My dearest reader,

You are simply amazing! Thank you so much for your support and readership! I can't tell you how much you reading this book means to me. I'm humbled and honored that you've dedicated your valuable time to experience the Unchipped universe with me. I'm still a newbie author, so if you were to leave me a review on the store you purchased this from, or Goodreads it would be a huge help! Short or long, doesn't matter. Reviews are the best way to help other readers find the Unchipped Series.

Want to stay in touch? I would love it if you'd subscribe to my newsletter:

@ www.TayaDeVere.com/HappinessProgram

You can also find me on:

Facebook .... @TayaDeVereAuthor

Instagram .... @TayaDeVere_Author

Goodreads .... @TayaDeVere

Bookbub .... @Taya-DeVere

Gratefully yours,
Taya

About the Author

Taya DeVere is a Finnish science fiction writer who loves telling stories about perfectly imperfect people in dystopian and postapocalyptic settings. Her characters are outsiders and rebels who stand up against injustice and form unlikely friendships with other rebels along the way. She is the writer of more than 21 books, and is always developing new stories to delight her readers. Taya's restless feet have taken her all over Finland, the United Kingdom, Spain, and North America. She lived in the United States for seven years but is currently based in Turku, Finland with her partner, Chris.

Best things in life: friends & family, memories made, and mistakes to learn from. Taya also loves licorice ice cream, secondhand clothes and things, bunny sneezes, salmiakki, and sauna.

Dislikes: clowns, the Muppets, Moomin trolls, dolls (especially porcelain dolls), human size mascots, and celery.

Taya's writing is inspired by the works of authors like Margaret Atwood, Peter Heller, Hugh Howey, and Blake Crouch.

Final Thanks

"I promise you, I don't need your cures or poorly thought-out pieces of advice, but I'll take free designer clothes, cheesecake, and a first-class plane ticket."
— **Keah Brown**

Writing William's story did not only take me back to California's sunny San Diego. This is where I hiked the most gorgeous mountain trails, came to know (and avoid) rattlesnakes and black widows, and burned my pale Scandinavian skin one too many times. No, William took me back to each state and city I've had the privilege to experience and live in during my seven years of adventure in the United States.

During these years, I met so many kind, funny, and unforgettable personalities. One of them is you, Bill. And not just because of that heavenly cheesecake assortment you brought us (okay, brought *me*) last time we sat down at a cookout and giggled like two sugar-high teenagers. Thank you for being such an amazing person. This world would truly be a different place if it was filled with more beautiful human beings such as yourself.

And as always, butt-loads of thank yous to my phenomenal editors Christopher Thompson and Lindsay Kaplan. Your professionalism, kindness, and patience leave me in a constant state of awe.

Also, special thanks to my irreplaceable proofreaders Laura Lennig, Luna Mrkovacki, and Chris DeVere. Your feedback and support keep me going strong.